"What did you say?"
Whitney gasped

Hawk winced at her obvious disbelief. "I said I love you. I'm too damn old for you, I have one unsuccessful marriage behind me, but I do love you."

Whitney still looked at him with suspicion. "I've always loved you, and I always will. And you let me go on thinking you were still in love with Geraldine!"

"Under the circumstances, it seemed the best thing to do—"

"Best for whom?" she exploded indignantly. "You? Because it certainly wasn't for me. I've been living in misery this past year thinking that you didn't want me in your life now that your duty was done! And what happens now?" She glared at him.

He shrugged. "I think that's up to you...."

CAROLE MORTIMER, one of our most popular—and prolific—English authors, began writing for the Harlequin Presents series in 1979. She now has more than forty top-selling romances to her credit and shows no signs whatsoever of running out of plot ideas. She writes strong traditional romances with a distinctly modern appeal, and her winning way with characters and romantic plot twists has earned her an enthusiastic audience worldwide.

Books by Carole Mortimer

HARLEQUIN PRESENTS
786—THE PASSIONATE LOVER
797—TEMPESTUOUS AFFAIR
804—CHERISH TOMORROW
812—A NO RISK AFFAIR
829—LOVERS IN THE AFTERNOON
852—THE DEVIL'S PRICE
860—LADY SURRENDER
877—KNIGHT'S POSSESSION
892—DARKNESS INTO LIGHT
909—NO LONGER A DREAM
923—THE WADE DYNASTY
939—GLASS SLIPPERS AND UNICORNS

HARLEQUIN SIGNATURE EDITION
GYPSY

These books may be available at your local bookseller.

Don't miss any of our special offers. Write to us at the following address for information on our newest releases.

Harlequin Reader Service
901 Fuhrmann Blvd., P.O. Box 1397, Buffalo, NY 14240
Canadian address: P.O. Box 603,
Fort Erie, Ont. L2A 5X3

CAROLE MORTIMER

hawk's prey

Harlequin Books

TORONTO • NEW YORK • LONDON
AMSTERDAM • PARIS • SYDNEY • HAMBURG
STOCKHOLM • ATHENS • TOKYO • MILAN

For John,
Matthew and Joshua

Harlequin Presents first edition February 1987
ISBN 0-373-10955-5

Original hardcover edition published in 1986
by Mills & Boon Limited

CHAPTER ONE

'AND if those threats were genuine, Whitney—which I think they are—you could lose a lot more than the story!'

She suppressed the shiver of apprehension that tingled down her spine at Martin's exasperated warning. She didn't doubt for a moment, either, that the threatening telephone calls she had received during the last week were genuine. The two made here to the newspaper had thrown her a little, but she had been working here two years now and accepted that very often the people involved didn't like the idea of a story being written about them; their displeasure was part of the territory. But the call she had received last night warning her off the Beresford family had shaken her up enough for her to mention it to Martin Groves, her editor at the daily newspaper she worked for. Last night's call had been made to her home, and she had an unlisted number!

'It's my story, Martin,' she maintained stubbornly, her chin raised challengingly.

'Bill could do just as good a job.'

'Better,' she acknowledged tightly, an angry flush beneath her high cheekbones. 'But it's my story,' she reminded him again tautly, not willing to accede to his demand that she pass her information on to someone else.

'Corruption in local councils has been covered before,' he dismissed scornfully.

'Maybe,' Whitney conceded abruptly. 'But I'm this close,'—she held the thumb and index finger of her left hand centimetres apart—'to proving that Tom Beresford is involved in most of it.'

Martin shook his head. He was a thin man with sparse grey hair, grandfather to a girl not much younger than the one seated before him. But even paternal pride couldn't make him claim that his granddaughter's beauty came anywhere close to Whitney Morgan's. From the top of her ebony head, her uptilted, violet coloured eyes, and ethereally lovely face, to the slender grace of her five-foot-seven body, she was a beauty. In the hard-bitten profession she had chosen for herself that beauty had been as much of a hindrance as a foot in the door. It was far from the only drawback he knew she had had to overcome.

'That close isn't close enough,' he told her harshly. 'I run a newspaper, not a suicide squad. I told you to lay off the Beresford story days ago,' he added sternly before she could interrupt.

She hadn't relished the idea of telling him about the calls, had expected this anger at the fact that she hadn't done as asked and dropped the story. But she hadn't been able to forget what she already knew, the fact that innocent people were being affected, incentive enough for her to ignore Martin's order, knowing he would be the first to congratulate her if she came through with a story for him.

'He's as guilty as——'

'Whitney, you know that old gangster joke about going for a swim with concrete shoes?' Martin cut in pointedly. 'Well Beresford wouldn't be joking,' he added drily, now that he had her full attention.

Whitney studied him warily, uncertainty in the wide violet eyes. 'You're just trying to frighten me,' she dismissed finally.

He sighed. 'Am I succeeding?'

'No!' she lied. Of course she was frightened!

He stood up forcefully. 'Whitney, the man is a barracuda! He wouldn't even bother to gobble you up himself, you're too unimportant and scrawny for him; he'd leave you to one of his minions.'

She knew exactly what Tom Beresford was like, knew that he ran an English version of the Mafia. In his early sixties, a big rough-diamond of a man, he ran an empire in England that was almost as powerful as the one across the Atlantic, although Whitney had found no connection to them during her investigation.

'I'm glad you told me that, Martin,' she laughed abruptly. 'I'm lunching with him today.'

'*What?*'

She winced at the expected reaction to her announcement. But if what Martin said about the concrete shoes was true she at least wanted someone to know who had been the last person she had seen! Martin looked ready to explode, though, his small wiry body tense with disbelief. Maybe she had been a little rash inviting Tom Beresford out to lunch, but with the security he had surrounding his privacy how else was she supposed to talk to the man himself? He had accepted the invitation, hadn't he! But after what Martin had just said she couldn't help wondering if they made concrete shoes in size five!

'I'm sure you heard me, Martin,' she sighed. 'We're meeting at the restaurant in twenty-five minutes.'

'Which restaurant?' His eyes were narrowed.

'Now, Martin——'

'I just want to make sure I have the right river dragged,' he told her blandly.

'There is only one river going through London,' Whitney chided drily at his effort to frighten her out of keeping the appointment.

'At least you had the sense to arrange to meet in town,' Martin scowled. 'What on earth possessed you to meet the man himself? Don't tell me,' he sighed resignedly. 'You wanted to give him the chance to defend himself!'

'He couldn't do that,' she said with certainty. 'But if I challenge him with what I already know he just might let something slip.'

Martin gave her a pitying look. 'How long did you say you've worked on the *National*?'

'Two years.' She told him what *she* knew he already knew, probably down to the day! 'I know, people like Tom Beresford don't let things slip out,' she sighed. 'I'm not completely stupid——'

'You could have fooled me,' he derided hardly. 'Just what are you hoping to achieve?'

Her eyes flashed deeply violet. 'I hope to show Mr Beresford that I'm not easily frightened off!'

Martin's expression softened at the disclosure. 'I admire your spirit, Whitney——'

'But you also deplore it!' she finished drily.

'It stinks,' he acknowledged tautly. 'Hawk will have to be told about this——'

'No!'

'Whitney——'

'I said no,' she bit out harshly, the thought of Hawk knowing about this sending her into a panic. She could just imagine his reaction.

'He owns the damned newspaper, Whitney,' Martin reminded her exasperatedly.

She was well aware of who and what Hawk was. And James Hawkworth – the last person to actually call him James was probably still trying to pick themselves up from the floor!—was not a man she wanted to get into an argument with. And she had no doubt that his reaction to what she was doing would be the same as Martin's. But for a very different reason.

'There's nothing to tell him——'

'One of his reporters receiving threats comes under the heading of something, Whitney,' Martin cut in determinedly. 'And I know Hawk is going to want to know about them. What did you say?' He looked at Whitney suspiciously as she mumbled something under her breath.

Her face was flushed as she looked at him challengingly. 'It doesn't matter.'

'It matters,' he bit out grimly. 'Although I can see you aren't about to repeat it. I just want you to know that my decision to take you off the story——'

'If you try to do that I'll go to another newspaper,' she told him stubbornly.

'Whitney!'

'I mean it, Martin,' she told him in a calm voice. 'I've worked too long and too hard on this one to just calmly let it go.'

He looked at her with narrowed eyes, sighing his defeat in the face of her determination. 'We'll see what Hawk has to say about it.' He maintained control of the situation with the threat. 'Maybe he'll decide that your pretty little body isn't worth saving,' he added grimly. 'Or maybe he'll agree with me that a reporter's life is worth more than a story!'

'Someone has to do something about Tom Beresford!'

'Then let the law deal with him!'

'They don't seem to be able to get the evidence on him.'

'And you do, I suppose,' Martin scorned.

She sighed, knowing she didn't have enough for them to print the story either. 'We both know what Hawk's answer is going to be,' she said disgustedly.

'Do we?' Martin taunted. 'I haven't noticed him leaping to your defence lately.'

Whitney felt her cheeks pale. She knew Martin was only being cruel to be kind when he mentioned Hawk's lack of interest in her recently, that he just wanted to shock her into realising what she was getting into any way that he could. But she was too sensitive of Hawk's dismissal of her from his life to feel anything but mortified about Martin's reference to it. Most of the people that worked on the newspaper knew of the history of her closeness to Hawk, but a lot of them had put it from their mind as Hawk continued to ignore her existence, seeming to accept that she was unconcerned with the situation, too. Only Martin had guessed how very much Hawk could still hurt her by his indifference.

'Tell him what you like, Martin,' she said wearily. 'I'm going through with my decision to meet Tom Beresford. If Hawk's the newspaper man that I think he is then he'll approve of what I'm doing.'

'And if he doesn't?' her editor grated.

She shrugged. 'That will be your problem.'

'Only until he catches up with you,' Martin warned derisively.

'As you just pointed out, why should he bother?' she dismissed bitterly, glancing frowningly at her wristwatch, diamonds studded about the slender gold face and strap, a twenty-first birthday present from Hawk the previous year. Her twenty-second birthday the previous month had passed without even receiving a card from him. She dismissed the memory impatiently, tossing back her mane of below shoulder-length hair to look at Martin. 'I'm going to be late if I don't leave now——'

'Whitney——'

'For goodness' sake, Martin,' she scorned, 'stop acting like an old woman.'

Anger flared in dark brown eyes at the taunt.

'Someone should have put you over their knee a bit more when you were a child!'

' "Someone" didn't dare,' she taunted.

'OK, Whitney,' he conceded wearily. 'Go to lunch with Tom Beresford. I'll be here to help pick up the pieces when you get back. *If* you get back,' he added softly.

A lot of her anticipation for the meeting had gone with Martin's disapproval of the idea; she had expected him to show a little more enthusiasm for what she had already achieved. No doubt the threat of Hawk's disapproval had a lot to do with his reaction, but he really needn't have worried; Hawk had made it obvious he no longer gave a damn what happened to her. But no doubt he would have something to say when he received the bill from the exclusive restaurant on her expenses! She could hardly have invited Tom Beresford to the local McDonald's.

She had dressed with great care that morning for her luncheon appointment, knew she was going to need all the cool poise she could muster to bluff her way through what she had insisted to Tom Beresford's assistant was a human-interest story. In view of the threatening telephone calls it was going to be a double bluff, Tom Beresford obviously knowing exactly what her interest in him was! But there were plenty of other things she could ask him about besides the local councils issue, one of them being his rise from the eldest son of a Yorkshire miner to a property and building tycoon who was rumoured to be under consideration for a lifetime peerage in the New

Year's Honours List next year for his contribution to British industry. If you were unaware of the corruption that had enabled him to make that meteoric rise in the building industry, then he did indeed appear a worthwhile candidate for the honour.

But Whitney had literally stumbled across his involvement with a councillor who had been sacked for taking bribes, and the deeper she looked into Tom Beresford's luck in receiving big building contracts from several of the councils, the more she had been convinced he was the one making the pay-offs. Six months of investigation had convinced her she was right. But she was going to need more than she had to convince Hawk to run the story; he only dealt in solid evidence, not beliefs.

She gave the *maître d'hôtel* her name once she reached the restaurant, allowing him to take her over to the table where Tom Beresford was already seated; she knew every inch of the man's lined and craggy face, had numerous photographs that she had taken during her study of him. But for today she was just another interested reporter; it wouldn't do to show she had instantly recognised him in the crowded room.

This morning her mirror had reflected back a coolly sophisticated young woman, her slender body shown to advantage in the pale lilac dress that made her eyes appear more violet than ever and gave a blue-black sheen to her loosely curling hair, its thickness cascading half-way down her back. Whitney was no fool, knowing that her

height gave her an advantage over a lot of men,
and with the three-inch heels on the black sandals
that she wore she knew she was going to tower
over Tom Beresford's five-foot-eight frame by a
couple of inches.

Her wish was granted as Tom Beresford
politely rose to his feet once the *maître d'hôtel* had
brought her to the table, and she smiled her
satisfaction as she shook his hand before sitting
down in the chair held out for her, ordering a
glass of wine at the query, the man seated
opposite her already having a glass of whisky in
front of him.

A quick glance at the table to the side of them
confirmed that Tom Beresford had brought along
Alex Cordell and Glyn Briant, the two men she
had learnt were his 'minders' or bodyguards, and
whom he preferred to call his 'associates'. She
had half expected the two men to be seated with
them, the two of them accompanying him
everywhere he went, but resisted the impulse to
ask him why they weren't and instead gave him a
brightly glowing smile. 'I've been looking
forward to this meeting,' she told him truthfully.

'Really?' Pale blue eyes looked at her coldly,
although his mouth curved in answer to her smile.

Whitney felt her control of the situation
slipping a little. Martin's comparison to a
barracuda had been wrong; this man was more
like a shark, watching and waiting before he
struck. But they were in a crowded London
restaurant, for goodness' sake; what could he
possibly do to her here!

She pushed the unsatisfactory—to her—answer to that to the back of her mind, giving him a guileless smile. 'Everyone likes to hear a success story, don't they?' she encouraged.

'Do they?' he drawled.

She gave a light laugh. 'You must know that they do.'

'Miss Morgan.' He spoke in a bored voice. 'What new angle on my success do you think you can come up with that the supplement of a —more prestigious—newspaper hasn't already covered?'

She had read the article that had been run a couple of months ago, had been amazed at the gullibility on the part of the newspaper. But that was half of Tom Beresford's success; the majority of people had no idea of the underhand methods he had used to get where he was. It was only if one dug deep enough, as she had, that the stench began to be apparent.

She gave him a sharp look as she thought the question over. Were the gloves to be taken off immediately then? No, she didn't think so; not yet, anyway. 'I write for a daily newspaper, Mr Beresford, with a circulation of two million a day. My story on you would run over two to three days.'

'I'm really not in need of the free advertising, Miss Morgan,' he drawled derisively.

Anger flared briefly in her eyes at his condescending tone before it was quickly dampened. Losing her temper with the man wasn't going to help one bit!

'Think of the New Year's Honours List,' she encouraged warmly. 'The story of the ingenuity and success of your enterprise can only encourage all those young people leaving school without any prospect of employment that there's hope for them after all.'

His mouth twisted sardonically. 'Flattery, Miss Morgan?' he mocked.

This man may once have been the 'rough diamond' she had thought him to be but the years had refined him, and his wealth had given him an arrogant confidence that was daunting. At sixty-two, he should have been paunchy and balding like Martin was, but Tom Beresford still had a head of thick silver hair, the very distinction of the style indicating the expensive cut, his body still lithe and athletic beneath the light grey suit and even paler grey silk shirt he wore. She was quickly learning, as he spoke with smooth assurance, that he was a man in complete control.

'Not at all, Mr Beresford,' she dismissed lightly. 'Your story could be uplifting for a lot of people.'

'I wasn't aware James Hawkworth ran stories like this in his newspaper,' he returned drily.

Whitney raised dark brows. 'I wasn't aware I had told you *which* newspaper I worked for.'

'You didn't,' he confirmed smoothly. 'A man in my position doesn't meet just anyone who telephones out of the blue claiming to be a reporter. I naturally did my homework on you.'

'Naturally,' she echoed tightly, knowing just

how intense that 'homework' had been. How *had* he got her unlisted telephone number?

'And of course Geraldine recognised your name straight away,' he added softly, his eyes narrowing as he waited for her reaction to the mention of the woman he had taken as his second wife after years of being a widower.

Geraldine. She still hadn't recovered from the shock of finding out that Geraldine was married to this man, couldn't begin to imagine how the other woman could prefer this man, for all his polished manner and wealth, to Hawk.

'It isn't exactly a common name,' she acknowledged tautly, thoughts of Geraldine always having the effect of making her hackles rise. How Hawk could still love the woman——? But he did, probably always would, even though she was now married to another man. Whitney didn't particularly want to be around when he was told she was doing an exposé on Geraldine's husband.

'After meeting you and witnessing first-hand your *un*common beauty I can quite understand Hawk's interest in you,' Tom Beresford murmured appreciatively.

Whitney stiffened at the unexpected—and unwanted—flattery. 'Didn't Ger—your wife— also tell you that's all over now?' she said tightly.

'You still work for him,' he shrugged.

'I'm treated like any other employee,' she defended hotly. *She* wasn't the one that was supposed to be on the defensive, damn it!

He raised thick silver brows. 'I had no idea

reporters earned enough money to be able to buy
themselves five-thousand-pound watches!'

She blushed. 'Mr Beresford——'

'I'm sorry, Whitney, that was a little personal
of me,' he held up his hands in apology. 'I hope I
can call you Whitney?'

'Of course,' she confirmed tautly, her eyes
flashing deeply violet.

'Shall we order?' he enquired softly, signalling
for the waiter as she abruptly nodded her consent
to the suggestion.

For all the notice Whitney took of her fresh
salmon salad it might as well have been the
tinned variety. She had felt, before meeting him,
that her in-depth knowledge of Tom Beresford
gave her the edge in this interview; she had soon
learnt how wrong she had been. Tom Beresford
was adept at only choosing to talk about the
things he wanted to, politely blocking off any
questions that went beyond that invisible barrier
he had erected. After almost an hour and a half,
when she watched him make his way through a
four-course meal and then coffee and brandy,
Whitney had had enough, not tasting any of her
own food in her agitation. And she was no nearer
to finding out anything about his involvement
with the local councils from his own lips than she
had been when she first made the connection six
months ago.

'Why don't you invite your bodyguards to join
us for coffee?' She deliberately antagonised him
in the hope of getting some reaction by
mentioning his two constant shadows.

Laughter in the pale blue eyes was not the reaction she had been hoping for! 'Glyn and Alex know better than to intrude on me when I'm in the company of a beautiful woman,' he drawled.

It was the second time he had called her beautiful, and Whitney found she didn't like the idea of this man finding her attractive.

'Don't worry, Whitney,' he assured mockingly, his eyes predatory. 'You can't become contaminated just by my acknowledging your beauty. That was what you were afraid of, wasn't it?' he taunted.

She became flushed at his correct assessment of her feelings. 'What did you——?'

'I'm sure Hawk must have complimented you on your beauty numerous times,' he cut in smoothly.

She gave him a frowning look. 'Could we leave Hawk out of this?'

'Of course,' he agreed easily. 'I don't exactly enjoy talking about my wife's previous lover.'

Whitney could have told him that had been in the plural rather than the singular, that Geraldine had never been satisfied with just one man in her life. But, like Hawk, he didn't look as if he wanted to hear anything derogatory about the woman he had fallen in love with after several years of grieving for his previous wife. What was it about Geraldine that inspired such love! Her father had always said Geraldine was a man's woman, and as far as Whitney was aware the other woman had never tried to inspire friendship among her own sex.

'Mr Beresford, what did you mean a few moments ago when you said I couldn't become contaminated by you?' She returned to what had bothered her about the statement; was it an admission of some kind on his part?

'You're the rich young socialite, I'm the son of a miner,' he shrugged casually. 'But I think over the years I've managed to eliminate most of my northern accent?' He met her gaze mockingly, seeming to guess that before meeting him she had expected him to be something of a country bumpkin, for all of his wealth and power.

'Obviously so,' she conceded with a cool nod, gathering up her bag and notebook. 'You've been very helpful, Mr Beresford, but I really do have to be going now.'

He gave an inclination of his head. 'I've enjoyed our little chat. I trust I'll see a copy of your story before it goes to print?'

Not the story she intended writing! 'Of course,' she nodded, indicating to the waiter that she would like the bill. She had felt that Tom Beresford had been laughing at her all during lunch, that he was probably finding the exorbitant prices for the meal at the restaurant of *his* choice highly amusing, too.

His hand reached for the bill first, meeting her questioning gaze with bland implacability. 'As I've enjoyed this meeting so much I insist on paying for our meal.'

Whitney blushed at his mockery, feeling more foolish than ever. Martin was going to fall off his chair laughing when she told him what a mistake this had been. 'The *National* can afford it,' she told him stiffly.

'I insist, Whitney,' he told her in a voice that brooked no argument. 'Please don't hesitate to contact me again if you need any more information for your article,' he invited derisively.

And I'll get you measured up for the concrete shoes, Whitney thought furiously as she left the restaurant after giving a mocking inclination of her head to the two watchful 'minders'.

The man had been pleasant, not a hint of a threat to his tone, and yet Whitney knew she trusted him even less now that she had actually met and spoken to him. Maybe it was the constant coldness of his eyes even when he laughed, or perhaps the complete assurance of his manner, as if he knew himself to be invincible, but she suddenly knew he was guilty of everything she thought he was.

She had too much of an uneasy knot in her stomach to feel jubilant at the knowledge, knew that she still had a long way to go before she had all the facts together, and that Tom Beresford had no intention of letting her write those facts. 'Know your enemy,' they said. Well, she knew hers now, and she wished that she didn't.

She knew that she had also been hoping for some sort of breakthrough, despite her denial earlier to Martin. But Tom Beresford was as likely to calmly hand over the combination of his safe as he was to deny or confirm her suspicions about him. Damn the man, he——

'Miss Morgan?'

'Yes——' She was prevented from turning
around to face the man who had spoken to her by
one hand being placed on her shoulder and the
other clamped about her wrist. 'What on
earth——?'

'Walk over to the car, Miss Morgan.' He
directed her towards a long black limousine with
darkened windows. So that she couldn't see out
or other people couldn't see in? 'Don't make a
scene,' the man urged as she began to struggle.

'Make a——! You can't do this to me!' she
protested indignantly. 'We're in the middle of a
crowded street!'

'I've already done it, Miss Morgan,' the man
told her with satisfaction as he urged her inside
the back of the car so that she stumbled slightly,
the door closing behind her before she could
straighten and face her accoster.

She frantically pulled at the door handle.
Locked! Her panic increased as she heard the low
purr of the car engine being started, banging on
the black glass partition between her and the man
now driving the car; she could see out of the
window after all, which meant no one was
supposed to see in!

The partition window lowered only enough for
her to be able to see the back of the man's head,
his hair thick and dark, a pair of enquiring brown
eyes meeting hers in the driving mirror. And as
Whitney had never bothered to take note of the
colour of eyes of Tom Beresford's two dark-haired
'minders' it could be either of the men driving
the car.

'Yes, Miss Morgan?' His voice was cajoling, as if he found the situation amusing.

'Stop this car immediately and let me out of here!' she ordered with a confidence that had long deserted her. She had been kidnapped, for goodness' sake!

'I'm sorry, I'm afraid I can't do that,' he shook his head.

Whitney sat forward on the edge of her seat, wishing she could see more of the man through the inch-wide gap at the top of the glass than the back of his head and a pair of amused brown eyes! The man was sick if he actually enjoyed abducting terrified women off the street and then watching them squirm. 'I——Where are we going?' she demanded weakly, her head starting to spin as the seriousness of what was happening to her washed over her. She was too young to die!

'Not too far,' he answered non-commitally.

They were driving towards the river! My God, Tom Beresford had been so incensed by her nerve in daring to question him the way that she had that he was getting rid of her right now!

'Look,' she moved closer to the glass, smiling at the eyes in the driving mirror, knowing he couldn't see her smile but hoping he could tell what she was doing by the warm expression in her eyes. 'I realise you're probably paid very well for doing this sort of thing——'

'Very well,' he confirmed softly.

She swallowed hard. 'I have some money of my own, enough to recompense you for letting me go, I'm sure. And look——' She desperately held up her wristwatch for him to see. 'This is worth a few thousand pounds.' God, he was actually smiling now!

'It's very nice,' he said disinterestedly, ignoring the watch after only a cursory glance.

Whitney breathed raggedly; how much was a life worth nowadays! 'I have other jewellery I can give you. And money. I'm sure I——'

'I've been paid to do a job, Miss Morgan,' he cut in patiently. 'And I always deliver.'

Oh my God! Whitney fell back against the black leather seat, random thoughts flitting through her brain in panicked succession. This couldn't actually be happening to her, it was like something out of an old Edward G. Robinson movie! And she would bet he had lost count of how many of his enemies had met this fate during his film career.

But prevalent in her thoughts was the knowledge that she would never have the chance now to tell Hawk how much she loved him.

Her heart sank even further as she saw they were rapidly approaching the Thames, her thoughts becoming hysterical now. Where did the man keep his supply of concrete? Maybe he would just tie a rock to her body and hope for the best.

Body . . .!

She couldn't just meekly sit back and meet her fate like this. This sort of thing just couldn't happen in the capital of England in broad daylight!

She sat forward so that she could meet the

man's gaze again, her heart pounding rapidly. 'Look, I think there's been some sort of mistake,' she began cajolingly. 'I'm not——'

'I've made no mistake.' He shook his head. 'I was told to bring Whitney Morgan here, and that's what I've done.' He had parked the car while they talked, climbing out now to open her door for her.

'Here' was a marina for luxury yachts. My God, they weren't going to dump her body here at all but take her out to sea and throw her overboard! She was not a strong swimmer and she knew she wouldn't stand a chance if thrown into the icy Channel. And the chances of her being picked up were about nil. Which was probably the idea.

Then she saw the name of the gleaming white yacht moored closest to her.

And the man watching her with narrowed eyes from the top of the gangway.

CHAPTER TWO

Two things became apparent to her at the same time, firstly that she wasn't about to be killed after all, and secondly that her driver hadn't been employed by Tom Beresford at all. The latter won out, the relief of the first realisation overshadowed by the anger of the second.

'You bastard!' she burst out furiously, hurling herself up the gangway without a glance for the distance between that and the murky water below. 'You unspeakable bastard!' The second accusation was accompanied by a powerful slap to one lean cheek.

Long slender hands came up to grasp both her wrists to ward off more blows reaching their target. 'Whitney——'

'I thought I was going to die!' she choked, her eyes misted with tears as she looked up at him. 'And it was you all the time!'

'Mr Hawkworth——'

Hawk glanced over her head at the driver as he stood hesitantly beside the car at the bottom of the gangway. 'It's all right, Peterson, I can handle Miss Morgan from here,' he assured the other man confidently.

Maybe it was that arrogance, or maybe she just didn't care what he thought of her behaviour after frightening her the way that he had, but suddenly she was kicking and scratching like a wild thing, Hawk unable to prevent all of the blows making contact, cursing under his breath as the pointed heel of her sandal caught him in the middle of the shin.

'So I see, Mr Hawkworth,' Peterson softly derided.

Tawny eyes, a clear golden colour, narrowed on him with displeasure. 'Just send me your bill,' he told the other man abruptly.

'There's nothing else I can do for you?' The other man lingered, obviously enjoying the show.

'Nothing,' Hawk grated, his eyes flaring with anger as he glared down at the still struggling Whitney. 'Stop it, you're making a damned fool of yourself!' he instructed through gritted teeth.

She stopped struggling only because she had run out of energy, knowing she wasn't the one to look the fool, he was! And looking foolish didn't sit well on the broad shoulders of James Charles Hawkworth. He towered over her now as he watched Peterson climb into the limousine and drive away, topping her five-feet-ten inches in the high-heeled sandals by at least four inches.

'Martin must have called you as soon as I left his office,' she muttered resentfully.

'He had better have done,' Hawk rasped with barely a movement of his lips.

Whitney glared up at him, resenting the fact that she had to do so. 'You scared me half to death,' she accused heatedly. 'I thought I was on my way to be fitted for a pair of concrete shoes!'

'That could still be arranged,' he told her with icy control.

'Don't you threaten me,' she snapped. 'I could still have you arrested for kidnapping.'

Hawk eyed her mockingly with those curiously gold eyes fringed by thick dark lashes. 'You're a little old to be called a kid!'

'Don't prevaricate.' She wrenched out of his hold on her arm, facing him now, wishing he didn't look quite so handsome in the open-necked white shirt and tailored white trousers, the Gucci shoes also white. 'You had me abducted in broad day——'

'On whose evidence?' He quirked brows the same dark colour as his lashes, his hair a dark blond with gold streaks among its thickness from the amount of time he spent aboard *Freedom* in warmer climates than the one in England; the name Hawk suited his colouring perfectly.

'Mine!' she claimed indignantly. 'And Peterson——'

'Oh, he wouldn't back up the kidnapping story,' Hawk denied with confidence.

Her eyes flashed. And to think that a short time ago she had been lamenting the fact that she hadn't had the chance to tell this man she loved him; she didn't love him at all, she hated him! 'I think you're overestimating your power of persuasion——'

'It isn't a question of persuasion, Whitney,' he mocked. 'I'm sure that where a man is concerned your accomplishments in that direction are much more successful than mine could ever be.' He made it sound like an insult. 'But Peterson believes your protests to have only been part of the game.'

Whitney's eyes narrowed. 'What game?'

'Shall we go inside?' he suggested with a pointed glance at the crew members standing about watching them curiously. 'If you're going to give another display like the one earlier I would rather it was a private showing.' He indicated that they should go into the lounge.

Whitney preceded him with a disgruntled scowl. She had been on *Freedom* several times in the past, and its elegant beauty didn't impress her at all at this moment, although she acknowledged that Hawk had refurbished the spacious lounge that was larger than a single floor of her house. She knew there was also a library and dining room on this upper deck, that below, the hundred-foot yacht also boasted six luxurious bedroom suites, as well as accommodation for half a dozen crew members. Hawk spent a lot of time on board, and as such the furnishing in leather, brass and glass was of a high standard; it was more than a home-away-from-home for him. Hawkworth House had never seemed as warm and welcoming.

'What game?' she demanded once more as he closed the door behind him, only the hum of the air-conditioning on this hot July day to disturb the silence; the crew were paid well to make themselves inconspicuous.

Hawk shrugged broad shoulders. 'You don't think Peterson—procures women for a living, do you?'

'He did a good job of abducting me,' Whitney maintained stubbornly.

Hawk limped over to the bar, drawing attention to the fact that she had bruised him earlier, taking a jug of the fresh orange juice he knew she liked from the fridge and pouring them both a glass. Whitney ignored hers once he had placed it on the glass-topped coffee-table, and with an indifferent shrug of his shoulders Hawk moved to sit down in one of the brown leather armchairs.

'Hawk!' she demanded impatiently as he sipped his drink, feeling suspiciously like stamping her foot at his infuriating behaviour, resisting the impulse with effort.

His expression softened, if a face carved out of granite could soften! He had the hard features that should only have appeared on a sculpture but were in fact flesh and blood, his cheekbones high, his cheeks fleshless, his mouth a hard, uncompromising slash. And those eyes could be just as hard and uncompromising, as they had been the day he walked out of her life.

'Peterson believes it's a game we play,' he drawled in a bored voice. 'You're the madly desirable woman and I'm the wicked abductor. Kinky, hm?' he derided.

'It's sick!' She dropped weakly into a chair, at last understanding the driver's amusement at her predicament, heated colour flooding her cheeks at how well she had played the supposed game. The man must think she was a pervert!

'Don't look so worried, Whitney,' Hawk

mocked. 'He assured me it wasn't the most unusual request he's received since he began his limousine service three years ago!'

'Just one of them!' she groaned her mortification.

'Oh, I don't know, the one about the sheikh who——'

'Hawk, I'm really not interested in the idiosyncrasies of an Arab too rich to have anything better to do than play ridiculous games!'

'No, maybe not,' he agreed slowly. 'That one did go a bit far. I was only trying to show you that Peterson didn't find anything unusual in our request——'

'Don't try and drag me into taking part of the blame,' she protested indignantly. 'I'll never be able to look the man in the face again!'

He quirked dark brows. 'Were you thinking of engaging his services in the future?'

'Hawk, all this is very amusing,'—her tone implied she thought it the opposite—'but it doesn't alter the fact that I almost had a heart attack when he made me get in the car. I felt so damned helpless, I didn't know what to do!'

'If Peterson had been a real kidnapper I would lay odds on you emerging the victor from the encounter!'

'Even though I realise there was no real danger I still don't feel very victorious,' she said shakily. 'I thought I was going to die,' she repeated breathlessly.

'And we both know why you thought that, don't we?' Hawk stood up in forceful movements,

having all the grace of a natural athlete when he
didn't have a bruised and aching shin, and
replaced the orange juice with a glass of whisky.
'I would have had Martin's job if he hadn't called
me when he did,' he revealed grimly. '*You* are
definitely fired!'

'You can't do that!' She stood up protestingly.

He raised his brows in cold fury. 'Forgive me,
as the owner of the *National* I thought I could.'
His tone was thick with sarcasm.

'That isn't what I meant and you know it,' she
said exasperatedly. 'You have no reason to sack
me, none that would stand up to the union
anyway.'

'How about persistent absenteeism?'

'I'm never off sick.' She shook her head, her
expression rebellious.

'I don't remember using the past tense,' Hawk
announced calmly.

Whitney blinked her surprise. 'You *have*
kidnapped me,' she said incredulously.

'Abducted,' he corrected smoothly. 'I don't
know of anyone who would pay a ransom for
you!'

'Beresford might,' she pointed out tightly.

His eyes flashed deeply gold. 'Maybe I should
telephone and ask him!'

She knew she had gone too far, had always
been able to tell that where this man was
concerned. Hawk wasn't a man to suffer fools
gladly, and by meeting Tom Beresford in the way
that she had Hawk considered her to be plain
stupid rather than just foolish! But carrying her

off the way that he had could have scared her to death, and she glared at him angrily. 'You can't keep me on board *Freedom* against my will——'

'Who says I can't?' he reasoned coldly. 'You've been on board the *Freedom* plenty of times before; why should anyone assume this time is any different?'

'Because I'm obviously a reluctant guest!' Whitney pointed out exasperatedly.

He gave an unconcerned shrug of his broad shoulders. 'I'll just tell them that you're loath to rest as the doctor has told you to.'

'You have an answer for everything, don't you?' she snapped irritably. 'And just what do you hope to achieve by this display of muscle?' she scorned.

'Achieve?' Hawk repeated with cold thoughtfulness. 'Maybe I'd just like to keep you alive for a few more years.'

'After presenting me with a diamond watch and kicking me out of your life a year ago——'

'I didn't kick you out!' he grated protestingly, his body taut with anger.

'Fulfilled your obligation, then,' she amended heatedly. 'It amounts to the same thing. After that I'm surprised you care one way or the other what happens to me.'

'Of course I care, damn you!' He glowered at her across the room.

Whitney gave a disbelieving snort. 'That's why you've been so solicitous of my welfare the last year, I suppose!' she derided.

'Martin would have let me know if anything

were bothering you; he told me you were doing fine,' Hawk dismissed with accusing impatience.

'Of course I'm doing fine, I don't need you to survive,' she claimed perversely. Hawk had always had this effect on her; she had resented it when he demanded to know her every mood, and she resented it just as vehemently when he seemed disinterested.

Hawk's mouth tightened. 'This time you just may do!' he rasped.

'You're as bad as Martin,' she sighed. 'I'm only following through a story, for goodness' sake.'

'On Tom Beresford.'

'Why is everyone so scared of the man?' Whitney scorned exasperatedly.

'It isn't a question of being scared of him, and if you weren't such a baby I'd tell you exactly why you should steer clear of this one,' he rasped.

'I don't think I was ever a baby,' she dismissed. 'Certainly not since I met you.'

A pulse jerked in his throat. 'Was living with me so bad?'

'Worse!'

'Whitney——'

'You know Geraldine is married to Tom Beresford now?' She inwardly cursed herself for asking the question as soon as it left her lips; of course Hawk would know who the woman he still loved was married to!

He gave a cool inclination of his head, a shaft of sunlight streaming through one of the windows picking out the gold highlights in his dark blond hair. 'I received an invitation to the wedding.' His bored drawl revealed none of his inner feelings.

'The bitch!' Whitney gasped incredulously, colour heating her cheeks as she realised she had just insulted the woman Hawk loved. 'I'm sorry. I——'

'It's all right, Whitney,' he derided drily. 'I was never blind to Geraldine's faults.'

But he loved her in spite of that. It had never made any sense to Whitney, this unquestioning love Hawk had for the other woman. In business Hawk had no peer, the *National* only one of his successes, and at thirty-seven he was more handsome than any one man had the right to be, his very coolness exuding a power and cynicism that was a challenge to every woman he met. And yet he threw away all that he had to offer on a woman who wasn't fit to be in the same room as him, let alone in his heart. It just didn't make sense to Whitney.

Of course some of her dislike of Geraldine sprang from her own love for Hawk, but she had detested Geraldine even before she had made the mistake of falling in love with Hawk. Mistake, because Hawk was the type of man to inspire the sort of love that would last a lifetime, and his heart belonged to Geraldine.

'Did you go to the wedding?' She gave a pained frown.

'Of course not.' His tone implied it had never even been a possibility. 'And watch some other poor devil go to his doom!'

Tom Beresford hadn't given the impression of chafing against his love for his wife when they had spoken earlier. Like Hawk, he gave the impression of granting her every whim and fancy.

'Tom Beresford isn't like you.' She spoke without thinking first, looking guiltily across at Hawk as she realised what she had said and how it must have sounded. 'I only meant——'

'I know what you meant, Whitney,' Hawk grated harshly. 'But you never understood my relationship with Geraldine. And I hope to God you never do!'

She wouldn't wish the mindless love Hawk had for Geraldine on anyone, and on this proudly arrogant man it was particularly unpleasant to witness. She had tried for a while to make a place for herself in his heart, but even though she didn't love or want him herself Geraldine had resented anyone else who did. For a long time she had managed to make Whitney's life a misery.

'Do you think Geraldine knows of Tom Beresford's method of business?' She watched Hawk closely for his reaction.

He shrugged. 'Geraldine never cared where the money came from as long as there was always plenty of it.'

Maybe if Hawk's love for Geraldine had been blind it would have given her hope in the past, but even knowing all the rotten things about Geraldine there were to know Hawk still loved her. That sort of love could never be ignored or overcome, it just continued to consume, like a sickness.

'You'll never be free of her.' Whitney spoke
her thoughts aloud without realising it, blushing
as she looked up awkwardly to meet his shuttered
gaze.

'Never,' he sighed.

'Hawk——'

'Whitney, let's drop the subject, shall we,' he
cut in forcefully, obviously wearying of the
subject. 'I had the *Freedom* brought up to
London with the intention of taking her out at
the weekend for a week or so. This has changed
my plans somewhat.'

'I don't see why,' she protested. 'If you'll just
let me go ashore——'

'No,' he bit out before she could finish. 'You're
staying right here until everyone forgets you were
doing a story on Tom Beresford.'

She remembered the predatory look in the pale
blue eyes of the other man and shook her head.
'That could take weeks,' she derided impatiently.

'You have weeks,' Hawk told her in a calm
voice. 'Months, if necessary. After all, you're
unemployed, and you don't have a cat to feed!'

'I——'

'And don't even think about carrying out your
threat to take this story to another newspaper,' he
added grimly, his eyes narrowed. 'If you attempt
to do that Martin will have to retaliate by quietly
spreading the word that the absenteeism story
was just that, that really you were sacked for
embellishing the facts to get a better story.'

Whitney paled, knew her career would be at an
end if such a rumour were ever started, however

untrue. 'I don't believe you would do that to me.'
She shook her head.

Hawk shrugged, his expression cold. 'Try me,'
he invited softly.

He had to know that a rumour like that, started
from such a reliable source as Martin Groves,
would finish her as a reporter forever. Not even a
provincial newspaper would employ her after
that. And she was damned good at her job. 'You
aren't doing this to protect me at all,' she accused.

'Who, then?' he grated harshly.

'Geraldine!' Her eyes were bright with anger.
'If her husband falls so will she! I don't believe
any woman could be that close to a man and not
know exactly what lengths he goes to to earn his
money!'

'No,' Hawk conceded. 'I'm sure Geraldine is
aware of every corruption her husband is
involved in.'

'Then——' She broke off as his expression
changed, blinking her confusion as he strode
purposefully across the room towards her.

'For God's sake, Whitney, I'm not going to hit
you!' he growled as she flinched, his fingers
biting into the tops of her arms enough to hold
her in front of him but not enough to actually
hurt her.

'What are you——?'

'Be quiet!' he grated, his head bending as his
mouth claimed hers.

All the breath left her body at the unexpected
caress, her limbs trembling as he moulded her
body to his, her senses quivering——

'I'm sorry, Hawk, I had no idea——!' The shocked voice of another man interrupted them.

Golden eyes gleamed their satisfaction before Hawk turned to look at the other man. 'It's all right, Stephen,' he assured smoothly. 'Whitney, you remember the captain of the *Freedom*?' He quirked dark brows at her.

She had met the other man several times during previous visits to the yacht, and nodded her head in greeting to him, now knowing the reason for Hawk's sudden—and devastating— kiss. She daren't even trust the steadiness of her voice to talk to the tall, distinguished captain!

Stephen Hollister still looked uncomfortable for having interrupted them at such an intimate moment. 'I can come back later.'

Hawk gave Whitney a hard look before nodding to the other man. 'Maybe that would be best,' he acknowledged. 'I was just about to escort Whitney down to her suite anyway.'

The innuendo in his tone was unmistakable, and with a rueful shrug of understanding the older man left them alone once more.

Whitney spun away from Hawk's side as soon as the door closed. 'And what if dear Geraldine got to hear about *that*?' she challenged, hurt by the way he had used her. Her worst humiliation was that he had to know she had responded to him.

His body tensed, his eyes as hard as the metal they resembled. 'My staff is paid very well *not* to gossip about me,' he bit out. 'Besides, none of them ever cared for Geraldine.'

She was so angry she just wanted to unnerve him the way he had disturbed her. 'And what about Mr Peterson?' she taunted. 'Was he paid to forget, too?'

'Yes,' he answered with simple arrogance.

'You didn't have to kiss me just now to shut me up,' she told him agitatedly, still able to feel the imprint of his lips on hers. 'A simple "someone's coming" would have sufficed! I know I lost my temper with you earlier but I'm not in the habit of causing a scene.'

'I know that,' he sighed wearily. 'I just—I'm sorry if I embarrassed you.' He shrugged awkwardly.

Embarrassed! She was a quivering mass of nerves, was still having trouble breathing, could barely resist the impulse to place her fingertips where his lips had touched hers; *embarrassment* was the last emotion she felt!

'You were my guardian for six years, shouldn't you be the one to feel embarrassed at being caught making love to me?' she scorned, to hide her complete devastation.

He drew in a ragged breath. 'Embarrassment doesn't come into it. You're right, I should never have kissed you. I'll have a word with Stephen and tell him to forget what he saw.'

'Don't forget to explain to him that the kiss you gave me couldn't possibly have meant anything when you still love your ex-wife!' Whitney's eyes were heavy with unshed tears.

'Whitney——'

'Don't bother to see me to my suite,' she told

him heatedly. 'I'm sure it's the same one that I usually occupy!' She closed the door forcefully behind her, resisting the impulse to lean weakly back against it, her back straight and unyielding as she took the stairway down to the deck that housed the suites.

She didn't relax that control until she had the door to the peach and pale cream suite firmly locked behind her; Hawk hated having people walking out on him in the middle of a conversation; she had learnt that at a very young age, having to spend every afternoon for a week of her holiday studying French the first time she had done it.

She had been fifteen when she had been put into Hawk's guardianship, when she had met him for the first time at all. She knew he and her father were friends, her father often speaking of him, and she had seen articles about the Hawkworth heir in the same magazines that wrote about her father.

At that time the two men had dominated the motor-cycle circuits, one of them always taking first place, the friendly rivalry inducing a lasting friendship. Whitney had known what her father did for a living, had been proud of his achievements from the safety of the boarding school he had sent her to when she was eight, her mother having died while she was still a baby. The day James Hawkworth arrived at the school in her father's place she had known Dan Morgan's sparkling career had come to an end on the race circuit he had loved so much.

The teachers at the school had managed to keep the knowledge of the fatal bike accident from her until Hawk arrived to gently break the news of her father's death, and because she had known of her father's close friendship with the younger man she had moved instinctively into his arms to cry over her loss. He had held her until the tears stopped, not speaking, just holding her, and then he had quietly explained to her that her father had left her care to him.

And so as well as her father's death she also had to contend with the fact that she had been left in the hands of a complete stranger. At first nothing had changed, Hawk leaving her at the school to finish her last year, the only difference there was being that instead of going home to her fun-loving father during the holidays she now went to the large imposing Hawkworth House in the exclusive part of London where Hawk and his wife lived.

Never having really known her mother, except from the photographs her father kept, Whitney had envisaged becoming friends with Geraldine Hawkworth. But the first time she met the other woman she had told her what a nuisance she was, and how her guardianship had disrupted her life. Whitney had always known that Hawk came from a very wealthy family, that he had become something of the black sheep when he had chosen to take up racing motor cycles instead of going into the family-run businesses that had made them all so wealthy. Being given the guardianship of a fifteen-year-old girl had necessitated Hawk donning the respectability of the family business rather than the excitement of travelling around the world racing, Geraldine had tartly informed her. And the other woman obviously resented the loss of that exciting life.

Not that Hawk had ever seemed to blame her in any way, not even when the change in career had such an adverse affect on his marriage. But for years the confinement of business had sat awkwardly on his shoulders, and Geraldine had never made any secret of her dissatisfaction with the new, staid, if equally rich, life she now led. The arguments between the couple had often been horrific those first two years after Whitney left school, Geraldine having a wicked temper.

When Whitney reached eighteen she had suggested to Hawk that now that his guardianship was over she should move out and give the married couple some privacy. It was then that she had discovered that, although she had now reached the age of consent, Hawk was to remain her guardian until she was twenty-one. Her father, perhaps because of his long absences, had always been protective of her, but nevertheless the thought of spending another three years with the bitter Geraldine and the determined Hawk had filled her with dismay.

But the situation between the married couple had suddenly changed. Geraldine began to go out alone, sometimes all night, and it was obvious when she returned the next morning in the same evening gown she had gone out in that she hadn't just arranged to stay overnight with friends.

Hawk became more withdrawn than ever, concentrating all his energies on his business empire, at last seeming to fit smoothly into this new career he had adopted for her sake, often working late into the evenings. Although the latter, Whitney had been sure, was so that he didn't have to be at home to witness Geraldine going out to meet what had to be her latest lover. Somehow the role of cuckolded husband didn't sit well on the shoulders of the man Whitney had come to know—and love. But, as Hawk raised no objection to the situation between himself and Geraldine, Whitney had had to accept that he loved the other woman, no matter what she did, or who she did it with.

Geraldine had finally tired of the life she was living just before Whitney's twenty-first birthday, asking Hawk for a divorce, which he agreed to give her without argument; how could he hold on to the woman when she obviously wanted to leave!

With Geraldine out of the house while they waited for their divorce, Whitney had tried to get closer to Hawk, to show him that she loved him even if Geraldine had been too stupid to. He had rejected her love by arranging for her to move into her own house, and handing over the diamond-studded watch on the eve of her birthday, the last time they had met before today.

She had been working for the Hawkworth-owned newspaper since she was twenty, and as she knew she was good at the job she had seen no reason to change that; she occasionally saw Hawk striding about the building. He looked older after his divorce from Geraldine became final and she remarried, more cynical than ever, and despite the fact that he had always appeared to be a highly sensual man there had been no women reputed to be in his life, not even casually. Even though she no longer wanted him Geraldine still owned him body and soul. It didn't matter to Hawk that she had made a fool of him with other men during their marriage, that she ridiculed his love during that stormy time, or that she had become involved with and finally married one of the most powerfully corrupt men in England.

Knowing Geraldine as Whitney did, only too well, and the other woman's craving for excitement in any shape or form—the more dangerous, the better she liked it—she had a feeling that Geraldine was involved in Tom Beresford's corruption right up to her beautiful neck.

She also had a feeling that, despite what the other woman had done to him, Hawk was going to protect Geraldine and the happiness she had found with the other man with the last breath in his body if necessary.

God, how she hoped she was wrong!

CHAPTER THREE

THE problem of what she was supposed to wear while on board the *Freedom* was resolved later that day when two suitcases containing all of her clothes were brought to her cabin by one of the crew. She hadn't given Hawk the key to her house!

She found him in the library, seated at the mahogany desk there, papers spread out before him. She firmly stood her ground as he looked up at her with a look designed to chill. 'Has breaking and entering become part of your accomplishments now?' she demanded accusingly.

He sat back in his chair, perfectly at ease as he unconsciously rolled the gold pen he held between his thumb and fingers. Whitney recognised the pen, she had given it to him for Christmas a couple of years ago. Hawk followed her line of vision, shrugging slightly. 'You have good taste.'

Not in everything. What sensible woman would fall in love with a married man, a man who had never shown her anything but the indulgent affection of an older brother. Except this afternoon when he had kissed her; there had been nothing brotherly about that! But he had apologised straight afterwards, and there was no memory of the caress in his eyes now.

She nodded abruptly. 'So do you.' She indicated the watch she wore. But like her his good taste didn't run to everything: his choice in women—Geraldine—was deplorable. 'But you didn't answer my question just now,' she added sharply. 'Did you break into my home to get my clothes?'

'No.'

'But——'

'I used the key, Whitney.' He indicated her capacious shoulder bag as it lay on a chair in the corner of the room. 'You left it behind earlier,' he explained.

Her eyes widened with indignation. 'And you just looked through it for my key?'

His eyes narrowed to golden slits. 'Do you have something in there I shouldn't see?'

Besides a few letters that she considered completely personal she also had the file on Tom Beresford and the photographs that went with it; she never allowed them out of her possession. Except when thrown into complete confusion by Hawk kissing her!

She snatched up the bag, holding it to her. 'That isn't the point and you know it. It's bad enough that *you* went through my handbag, but the thought of some stranger going to my home——'

'I went and got your things myself, Whitney,' Hawk put in softly.

She didn't know which was worse, the complete stranger or Hawk viewing the home she had made for herself at his request! She didn't

live in the fashionable part of London; the three-
storeyed house was Victorian, and she had
quickly stamped her own personality on the
rooms. There were also a lot of pictures of Hawk
about the house, although thankfully a lot of
them were coupled with her father and so may
not have raised Hawk's suspicions as to why she
should have photographs of her ex-guardian in
her new home.

'At least that's something,' she snapped, to
cover up her feelings of awkwardness. 'But why
couldn't you have just *asked* for the key?' She
scanned the contents of her bag.

'Don't worry, there's nothing missing,' Hawk
grated at her suspicion.

'Not even the key to my house?' she scorned,
her eyes blazing deeply violet.

'I returned it once it had served its purpose,'
he bit out.

'Now nice of you!'

'Would you rather have worn that same dress
for the next few weeks?' he rasped.

Her mouth tightened. 'I'd rather go home and
continue with my story.'

'No.'

His tone brooked no argument and from
experience Whitney knew he was adamant. 'What
am I supposed to do here all day; I'll be bored out of
my mind!' she protested at her confinement.

'You've never been bored on the *Freedom*
before,' he shrugged.

'I've never been held prisoner on board
before!'

His expression darkened. 'You aren't a prisoner now, either; you just aren't free to leave!'

'I like your distinction,' she scorned.

Hawk sighed. 'You're free to move about the yacht as much as you want——'

'Thanks!'

'I'm beginning to see why parents ask the question, "where did I go wrong?" so much,' he snapped. 'There wouldn't be any need for this at all if you would just do what you're told. But we both know you've never been very good at doing that, don't we?'

She blushed, knowing he was referring to the time she had decided to go on holiday with a group of friends against Hawk's wishes and almost paid for her stubbornness by being raped when she refused to join in the bed-swapping games the others found such fun. Hawk had found her sleeping on a bench at the sea-front. Not once had he said, 'I told you so', seeming to realise she had suffered enough from the disillusionment at her so-called friends. Until now.

'This isn't the same thing——'

'I agree; then it would only have been your virginity you lost!'

He was furious, and she knew that she would be wise to stop while she could emerge from the conversation with some degree of dignity. But she couldn't seem to help herself. 'What makes you so sure I even had that to lose?' she challenged.

'What makes you think I cared?' he bit out cruelly.

Whitney flinched, getting no more than she
had expected. She gave a shaky sigh. 'I'm sorry.
All that was uncalled for.'

'I'm glad you realise it.' He wasn't so easy to
forgive. 'Now, would you prefer it if I took your
clothes back to your home——'

'Of course not.' All the fight had momentarily
gone out of her. 'I'll need them if I'm going to be
on here for any length of time.'

'There's no "if" about it,' Hawk rasped.

Whitney knew she had to retreat now, Hawk
too coldly angry to be the one to back down.
'Then in that case I hope you packed a bikini; I
can at least get a suntan if nothing else.'

'No sunbathing.' Hawk shook his head.

Her eyes widened. 'Why on earth not? I can
assure you that I don't intend flirting with any of
the crew!' she claimed indignantly.

His mouth tightened. 'The men are too loyal to
me to do anything about it even if you did,' he
drawled confidently. 'They know, from Stephen
on down, that it would cost them their job. When
I told you earlier that you could move freely
about the yacht maybe I should have said *inside*
it. I don't want you out on deck where you're
visible.'

'To who?' she demanded incredulously.

'Anyone who happens to be interested!'

Whitney frowned at his vehemence. None of
this was in character for Hawk. He was always
calm, always in control, he never lost his temper
the way that he had today. Something about all of
this had definitely unsettled him. 'You can't

believe I'm really in some sort of danger?' she derided dismissively.

'You were the one that received the telephone calls. What do you think?' he reasoned hardly.

Her face paled as she recalled that un-recognisable, softly threatening voice. It had belonged to a man, but the husky softness of the tone had made it impossible to identify. Nevertheless, the threats had sounded genuine enough, too much so for her peace of mind. 'Does this mean Tom Beresford gets away with this?' she groaned.

'Not necessarily,' Hawk answered non-com-mittally. 'Martin tells me you have a file on the man, photographs too.'

Whitney looked at him searchingly, not quite trusting the blandness of his tone. 'What about it?' she asked warily.

'If you give it to me I could go through it, see what you have.'

There was still something about his calmness that made her uneasy. 'The file on Tom Beresford is at the house,' she lied, a guilty blush colouring her cheeks. She took an involuntary step backwards as Hawk stood up.

His eyes narrowed at the guilty movement as he sat back on the edge of the desk-top. 'That's a pity,' he said slowly, his head tilted at a questioning angle.

She didn't like the way he said that. 'We could always go and get it,' she suggested eagerly.

'I don't think so.' He shook his head.

'Hawk——'

'It's getting late, Whitney, why don't you go and change for dinner.'

She chewed on her inner lip. She hadn't seen Hawk to talk to for almost a year, and yet she couldn't believe he had changed so much, aloof from her in a way she had never known before. Until she was eighteen and his marriage to Geraldine had deteriorated beyond the point of no return, he had been kind to her in a paternal way. Now he was just plain distant!

'Formal or informal?' she asked absently, still puzzled by the change in Hawk.

His mouth quirked. 'Sean would say formal, I would prefer to lounge.'

Her eyes lit up at the mention of the other man. 'Sean is still with you?'

Hawk raised dark brows. 'Shouldn't he be?'

The fiery Irishman had been Hawk's chef ever since she could remember, looking more suited to being an engineer in the navy than the master chef that he was, a big jovial man with a loud voice and the kindest blue eyes Whitney had ever encountered. It wasn't that she was surprised he was still with Hawk—the majority of his staff were very loyal, which was why she didn't doubt for a minute Hawk would be able to keep her aboard the *Freedom* for as long as he wished—it was just gratifying to know there was one friendly face on board. Sean had taken her to his heart the moment they first met.

'It will be nice to see him again.' She smiled her pleasure.

Hawk grimaced. 'I wish we had all been

awarded that same eagerness,' he said drily, touching his cheek ruefully where she had hit him with such force earlier.

Whitney gave him an unsympathetic look. 'Maybe next time you'll realise a simple invitation would have achieved the same result!'

'That wasn't the impression Martin gave me,' he derided drily. 'He said you were issuing challenges to anyone who would listen to them. And that you were casting aspersions on my discipline of you as a child.' He quirked dark brows mockingly.

It hadn't been Hawk she had been referring to at all, and Martin knew it, damn him. 'I think I'll buy Martin a wooden spoon for his next birthday,' she grimaced.

Hawk laughed, the first time she had seen him do so in a very long time, and she was fascinated by how much younger he looked, the frown gone from between his eyes, looking almost boyish as he continued to grin at her. 'Send it from both of us, will you,' he said warmly. 'I'm sure he passed on that last piece of information as much to annoy me as to get you into trouble.'

'Probably,' she acknowledged ruefully. 'Maybe sending him out on a few assignments would be better than the wooden spoon!'

'Now that's cruel!' They both laughed at Martin's aversion to leaving his desk.

She had been abducted, was even now being held on board this yacht against her will, and yet at this moment she didn't care, knew she could stand anything if she could be with Hawk.

'Where were you thinking of cruising?' she asked
breathlessly.

'Just around the Med for a few days,' he
shrugged, his humour fading.

'That sounds nice.' Her eyes glowed at the
prospect of being alone with him. They had only
ever been alone on *Freedom* in the past, this the
one place Geraldine refused to bring her caustic
presence. Maybe Hawk would finally see that she
was no longer a child.

He nodded abruptly. 'Once we're out at sea
you can go out on deck.'

'In my bikini?' she teased.

He looked at her steadily for several minutes,
his gaze seeming to move reluctantly over the
smoothness of her curves beneath her dress. 'If
that's what you want.' He turned away, standing
up to move back around the desk and sit down.
'I really do have to finish up here before
dinner . . .'

She took the dismissal for what it was,
although she refused to be daunted. Maybe her
time on here wasn't going to be so bad after all.
And as soon as they got back to London she
intended continuing with the story on Tom
Beresford. It had waited all these months for
exposure; a week out of time with Hawk wasn't
going to make much difference.

All her resentment at his high-handed
treatment of her had gone by the time she joined
him for dinner later that evening, feeling pleased
with her appearance, knowing the black gown
gave her a sophistication Hawk never seemed to

have associated with her, her hair loose and flowing.

But her own appearance was forgotten as soon as she looked at Hawk, her heart beat rising in tempo at how sexy he looked dressed in black, too, his shirt casually unbuttoned at the throat. No man should be allowed to be this handsome!

'You look beautiful,' he told her huskily.

'So do you' didn't quite sound appropriate—even if he did! 'I'm glad I realised that your idea of "lounging" didn't mean jeans and a T-shirt,' was her only reference to how devastating he looked.

He gave a rueful glance at the candlelit table behind them. 'It seems I wasn't quick enough earlier to stop Stephen gossiping with Sean.'

Delicate colour heightened her cheeks. 'I don't mind,' she assured him gruffly.

'No?' he quirked dark brows.

'I—er—I mean, of course, if you don't,' she said awkwardly, inwardly cringing at the way she had handled the intimacy. 'And why should you?' she added more confidently. 'As you said, Geraldine isn't likely to find out.' She winced as she mentioned the other woman's name, could have kicked herself as Hawk's expression became withdrawn.

'Could we not talk about Geraldine tonight?' he finally rasped.

She didn't care if she never heard the other woman's name again! 'Fine by me,' she agreed dismissively. 'I wonder what Sean has prepared us for dinner?' she asked conversationally.

Hawk's mouth twisted. 'Knowing you were on board, probably your favourite pâté and beef Wellington, and to hell with what I like!'

She laughed softly at his teasing, his hand gently on her back as he guided her over to the table. 'That was before I had to watch the calories!'

He frowned at her across the width of the table, the small oak oval that Sean had obviously decided was perfect for the intimate dinner he was preparing them. 'Your figure is perfect,' Hawk grated. 'It always has been.'

'Ah, but it won't stay that way if I indulge in too much of Sean's cooking.'

'And what's wrong with my cooking, I'd like to know?' Sean joined them from the galley below, placing the plates of pâté before them; he was wearing jeans and a T-shirt, his only concession to his station the starched white hat on his head.

'Nothing—that's the trouble!' Whitney grinned at him. 'It's good to see you again, Sean.'

'You, too, darlin'.' He smiled down at her, only needing tattoos on his hands and arms to look like a merchant seaman. He had been horrified when Whitney had suggested it to him, claiming his hands and his arms were his tools-in-trade, and much too valuable to be so abused. Considering the king's ransom Hawk paid him, perhaps he was right! He also cooked and presented the best food Whitney had ever tasted. 'I'm glad to see Hawk's finally come to his senses and seen you for the beauty you are,' he continued with his usual candour. 'If he hadn't have done I may have snapped you up myself.'

'Sean——'

'I wish you had told me, Sean.' Whitney feigned dismay, ignoring Hawk's narrow-eyed look at her interruption. 'I've been waiting for you to propose for years, and now it's too late.'

'Ah, and there's the way of it then.' He shook his head morosely, falling in with her game, a mischievous twinkle in his eyes. 'Still, if it couldn't be me you couldn't have chosen a better man than Hawk.'

'I'm glad you approve.' She smiled at him warmly, Hawk scowling now.

'And what's wrong with you, me lad?' Sean gave him a piercing look. 'Dazed by your good fortune, I bet,' he said knowingly.

'Something like that,' Hawk drawled.

Sean nodded, as if pleased with the answer. 'If you ever get tired of him, Whitney love, remember there's always Sean O'Gilligen. I'd be good to you.'

'I'll bet,' Hawk muttered as the other man went back down to his galley. 'You shouldn't have encouraged him, Whitney.' He frowned at her.

She shrugged, spreading pâté on her toast. 'I've always joked about with Sean like that, it doesn't mean a thing.'

'I meant about us,' Hawk grated. 'The less people who believe that the better.'

All the enjoyment suddenly went out of the evening. 'Because of Geraldine.'

'Because I was your guardian for six years, damn it!' He glared.

'And now I'm twenty-two and all grown up!' She glared back at him.

'Not that grown up!' he rasped.

They ate their pâté in stony silence, Whitney unable to believe how Hawk could be so bloody-minded about what was, after all, just a bit of fun. He knew as well as she did that the rumour about the two of them would go no further than the *Freedom*; the men that worked for him on board were fiercely loyal, even without the financial inducement.

Only Geraldine had been immune to the loyalty Hawk evoked, spending his money, using his power, but giving him very little in return; the two of them hadn't even shared a bedroom the last three years of their marriage. Hawk had acted as if the enforced celibacy didn't bother him, but it must have been a terrible blow, considering his continuing fidelity, when Geraldine had told him she wanted a divorce so that she could marry the man who had been her lover for several months.

'Sad thoughts?'

She looked up from her beef Wellington to find Hawk watching her frowningly. 'I can't re-member,' she avoided awkwardly.

'Strange,' Hawk drawled disbelievingly. 'I can never remember your having a lapse of memory like that before.'

She blushed at the taunt. 'Then it should tell you that my thoughts were private,' she snapped, wincing as she realised just how awful that had sounded. But how could she tell him she had been wishing she could have eased his celibacy all those years! 'I'm sorry,' she told him regretfully.

He nodded abruptly. 'We've grown so apart this last year,' he realised ruefully. 'Do you realise that today when I picked up your things was the first time I've actually seen your home?'

'You've been invited—I'm sorry.' Once again she regretted her caustic tone—he had received enough of that from Geraldine over the years! 'You're a busy man——'

'Never too busy for you, Whitney.' He placed his hand on hers on the table top. 'I'm always here if you should need me.'

She always needed him. This last year without him had seemed never-ending, the few invitations she had initially made to him to visit her so gently rebuffed at first that she hadn't realised what was happening. And then his refusals hadn't even been politely made any more, and finally she had stopped asking, realising that the part of his life that had contained her had been irrevocably closed.

'What did you think of my home?' she asked lightly, not encouraging another rejection.

His mouth quirked. 'An interesting concept,' he remarked slowly.

Whitney laughed at his tactful answer. 'You didn't like it!'

'Having the bedrooms downstairs and the living area upstairs threw me a bit,' he acknowledged drily. 'But I soon found my way around.'

She had taken one look at the old house, fallen

in love with it and its location, and decided that it was designed completely wrong inside. A few minor changes and it was perfect.

'Is it a new fashion?' Hawk still seemed a little dazed by her upside-down idea of living.

'I don't think so.' She shook her head. 'I just prefer it that way. After all, what's the use of having those lovely views from the top of the house if you only go up there to sleep?'

'There is that,' he drawled.

'You're laughing at my logic,' she said without rancour.

'Maybe a little,' he conceded lightly. 'I've just never thought of it like that before.'

'But can't you see——'

'I can,' he said dazedly, a little bewildered by his own sense of understanding the upside-down design of her home. 'It might be different if you had a garden, but as you don't I can see that it would be more comfortable the way that it is.'

She nodded. 'It's also more private. I don't need to draw the curtains at all in the lounge because no one can see in at me.'

'As I said, it's an interesting concept,' Hawk drawled drily.

'But not something you would want at Hawkworth House,' she realised mockingly.

'Well I do have a garden,' he reasoned. 'And Rusty might get a little confused if I started messing around with his living arrangements.'

She smiled at the mention of Hawk's red setter. 'How is he?'

'Getting old, like the rest of us,' he sighed.

Whitney frowned. 'He isn't ill, is he?'

Hawk shook his head. 'Just more temperamental than ever. I don't think fatherhood agrees with him,' he added derisively.

Her eyes widened. 'Rusty is a father?' She had thought he was getting too old for that.

Hawk laughed softly at her stunned expression. 'He got to Mrs Russell's Honey before the male golden labrador she had picked out for her baby! She wasn't in the least amused when she saw the pups!'

Remembering Hawk's snobbish next door neighbour at Hawkworth House, and the almost fanatical way the other woman had protected her dog, Honey, she guessed that was probably a slight understatement. 'I bet they were adorable.' She smiled at the imagined pups.

'Mrs Russell didn't think so, but she managed to find homes for them all. Rusty isn't too thrilled by the presence of his son and heir!'

'*You* bought one,' Whitney realised excitedly.

'Oh no, Mrs Russell gave me the choice of the litter,' he said, tongue-in-cheek. 'She also told me I had better have one or she would send Honey over to dig up the prize roses!'

The conversation flowed more easily between them after this nonsense, so that by the time Whitney said good night she felt as if she and Hawk had reached at least some sort of closeness again. The paternal kiss he gave her on her forehead before they parted told her it wasn't the sort of closeness she would have liked!

But it was more than she had had from him the

last year, the knowledge that he was only feet away from her in his own suite down the corridor making it impossible for her to sleep.

After lying awake for some time not even feeling sleepy she decided to go back up to the library to get a book to read, Tom Beresford and her story on him far from her mind as she thought of the days ahead with Hawk. It was going to be so good being with him again, although Hawk couldn't guess that she was going to use this probable last chance with him to try and make him see her as a woman. If she failed when completely alone with him, then she might as well give up!

'. . . we shouldn't be disturbed in here.'

Whitney froze as she heard Hawk enter the adjoining lounge—and he obviously wasn't alone. What was he doing wandering about the yacht at one o'clock in the morning? And who could possibly be calling on him at this time of night that he didn't want to be disturbed with? The realisation that it was probably a woman, possibly even Geraldine Beresford, kept her seated in the chair.

'No one saw you come on board?' His question was accompanied by the chinking of glasses as he poured himself and his guest a drink.

'No one,' his visitor confirmed. 'I'm not some rank amateur!'

It was a man's voice! And it sounded vaguely familiar. Whitney strained to hear their hushed voices now.

'I had to leave a couple of men on deck,' Hawk

sighed. 'You know Whitney is on board? I had no choice,' he protested as the other man gave a disapproving snort. 'She was getting too inquisitive.'

'He certainly didn't like seeing her at lunch today,' the other man acknowledged grimly.

My God, Whitney realised, this man was involved with Tom Beresford. And Hawk?

'I'm not going to let him or anyone else hurt her,' Hawk grated. 'She's just a child who doesn't realise what she's become involved in.'

'I don't think he quite sees it the same way,' the other man drawled. 'And he's going to be very wary when he finds out she's staying here with you.'

'Whitney was my ward, she works for me,' Hawk scorned dismissively.

'It's the last part that seems to be bothering him. It's making him unsure of you. And we can't have that, not after all the work we've done.'

'Now look, Glyn——'

Glyn? Glyn Briant, one of Tom Beresford's 'minders'? Whitney felt sick and bewildered. It couldn't be because Hawk was involved with Tom Beresford that he wanted her story stopped; she couldn't believe that! And yet what else could all this mean?

'Does she have the file and photographs with her?' the man called Glyn asked impatiently.

Hawk sighed. 'She says not, but I searched her home earlier and I know they aren't there. By the time I realised they were probably in her bag all the time it was too late to prevent her taking it back. Unfortunately, I *am* an amateur!'

'That's all he's really interested in from her,' the other man said grimly. 'But until he gets them your ward is a hindrance he doesn't need. Needless to say I'd like to take a look at them, too,' he added interestedly.

'When I agreed to come in on this I specified that Whitney was never to be involved——'

'Hawk, she involved herself,' the other man rasped. 'She was warned off, but she just kept coming. And you know that there are too many other people who could get hurt for us to back off now. If you can give him what he wants, maybe he'll forget all about Whitney Morgan.'

'OK,' Hawk sighed, 'I'll get the file and photographs for you.'

'And what are you going to do with Miss Morgan in the meantime?'

'Take her to the Med for a few days and hope he forgets her, as you said,' Hawk grated grimly.

'A few days, even a few weeks, wouldn't be enough time for that,' the other man muttered. 'She's been making herself too visible lately.'

'Then just what do you suggest I do?' Hawk rasped, obviously not expecting the other man to have a solution either, swearing softly under his breath as the other man seemed to take his time thinking about it.

'Maybe if we could show him that Whitney is harmless,' Glyn finally said slowly.

'And how do you propose to do that?' Hawk demanded impatiently. 'I had her editor order her off the story six months ago, and yet she went right on with it.'

'And now he's as jumpy as a kitten!'

Tom Beresford, jumpy? If he had been at lunchtime, he had hidden it well!

'We've come too far, risked too much, to screw up this deal now,' Hawk bit out.

'We aren't going to screw it up,' the other man told him with cool confidence.

'We are if I lose the little trust I've gained with him. He's already so damned wary.'

'Wouldn't you be, especially with this latest development?'

'Whitney is my responsibility, I'll handle her,' Hawk announced arrogantly.

'Will you?'

'Yes!'

'She doesn't come over as a young lady that likes to be "handled",' Glyn Briant mocked.

'She'll do as I tell her,' Hawk told him fiercely.

'I hope you're right,' the other man murmured. 'I haven't come this far to lose out because a little girl got too nosey!'

'You won't,' Hawk assured him grimly.

'Cancel this trip to the Med for a while, will you,' the other man instructed. 'I don't think it would look too good if the two of you sailed off into the sunset right now!'

'There's nothing like that between Whitney and I,' Hawk grated harshly.

'Do you think Geraldine is going to believe that?' the other man scorned.

'Who the hell ever knows *what* Geraldine thinks?' Hawk dismissed impatiently.

'And how can she really object, in the circumstances?' the other man taunted.

'I don't like Whitney being involved, Glyn,' Hawk bit out abruptly.

'We don't have a choice,' the other man told him arrogantly. 'She's got herself caught in the middle, and she'll have to take her chances like the rest of us.'

'If she becomes suspicious——'

'Then you'll *have* to handle her,' Glyn told him icily. 'No one else has to know we're involved in this deal. And we have to get it moving soon. Lives depend on it.'

'Whitney——'

'Nothing will happen to your little ward as long as you can convince him she's under your control. And in the meantime, get those photographs and the file; at least they give us something to barter with!' he assured Hawk impatiently.

Whitney couldn't hear any more of the conversation as the two men continued to talk in hushed voices as they left the lounge, Glyn Briant obviously leaving. Lives depended on Hawk making some deal with Tom Beresford? *Hawk's* life?

CHAPTER FOUR

WHITNEY felt as if she sat across the table from a stranger at breakfast the next morning. The Hawk who could become involved with the shady dealings of a man like Tom Beresford wasn't the same man who had taken her into his home seven years ago and shown her a kindness that had made her love him. But then that Hawk wasn't the same man who had dismissed her from his life a year ago either, his duty over, his affection removed.

When had he changed so dramatically? *Why* had he changed? She had always assumed, with the considerable business holdings the Hawkworth family had when Hawk took over the running of them seven years ago, that he must have continued their success. He always gave the impression that he had. But she had gone over and over in her mind what the reason could be for Hawk dealing with a man like Tom Beresford and the only conclusion she could come up with, that sounded at all feasible, was money. And she felt responsible if that were true. Hawk had given up the career he loved and was successful at, to become the respectable businessman worthy of her guardianship, and if he had failed at the task and lost all the Hawkworth money then it was her fault. He had probably lost Geraldine for the same reason, the other woman not the type to have patience with failure, especially if it meant there was no longer as much money available for her to spend.

Although none of this really justified Hawk's involvement with Tom Beresford. And the other man, from the conversation she had heard between Hawk and Glyn Briant the night before, obviously wasn't completely convinced either, hence Hawk's urgent need to prove himself.

When had Hawk changed from that reservedly affectionate man she had always loved to become as corrupt as Tom Beresford, a man she despised?

'You're very quiet this morning?'

She looked up with a guilty start, avoiding Hawk's direct gaze, too disillusioned by what she had heard to look at him and not show the emotion. 'I didn't sleep all that well,' she told him truthfully, sleep eluding her completely after what she had overhead.

He nodded understandingly. 'It's always a little strange the first night on board, even when you aren't moving!'

Last night hadn't been strange, it had been devastating! Tears misted her vision.

'You'll be pleased to know,' Hawk continued casually, 'that I've decided to stay on in London for a few more days.'

She swallowed hard. 'That means we aren't going to have our trip around the Med?'

'You weren't that keen on going anyway,' he chided lightly.

She was now, though! Hawk hadn't actually become actively involved with Tom Beresford's corruptive methods yet, and if she could get him away on her own and try to persuade him he would be making a mistake if he was tempted by that easy money then she would gladly give up the story on Tom Beresford. Anything, to stop Hawk's involvement.

'It would be fun, Hawk.' She looked up at him beseechingly, her hand on his arm.

He avoided her gaze this time. 'Something has come up,' he told her abruptly. 'I have to stay on here for a while. In fact, I'm going into town now so why don't you go back to bed for a while; you look washed out. I'll leave instructions for you not to be disturbed.'

How could she be anything else but disturbed when Hawk was contemplating personal suicide!

'I'll pick up the file and photographs on Tom Beresford from your house for you if you like,' he added casually.

All the breath seemed to be knocked from her body at the suggestion. She couldn't give him the file now even if she wanted to, not when she knew he was going to use it to barter to his destruction. 'I—er—I think it's in my desk,' she lied, moving her feet slightly to touch her bag reassuringly as it lay next to her chair, the file and photographs nestled inside seeming to burn at the touch.

'Whitney——'

'I——Oh, damn!' she protested regretfully after deliberately knocking her orange juice all

over him. 'I'm so sorry, Hawk.' She watched as
he mopped ineffectually at the juice as it rapidly
stained his dark trousers. 'That was very clumsy
of me.'

'It doesn't matter,' he dismissed with a
grimace. 'I can easily go and change.'

The respite was what she had been hoping for,
and she relaxed back with a sigh of relief once
Hawk had gone to his suite, giving up all
pretence of trying to eat the toast she had
buttered to accompany her juice, spooning sugar
into a cup of strong coffee instead, and drinking
it down thirstily. She didn't know how she was
going to cope with this, felt like crying and
screaming at the same time. She had to stop
Hawk, she just had to! But how? He could be
going off for a meeting with Tom Beresford right
now.

'Sorry I was gone so long.' He rejoined her ten
minutes—and three cups of coffee for Whitney—
later. 'The orange juice had made me sticky so I
took a quick shower.'

He looked so handsome to her this morning,
the fitted brown trousers and shirt complemented
perfectly by the brown sports jacket with its fine
gold check, his hair looking more gold than dark
blond.

He wore tailor-made clothes, silk shirts, hand-
made shoes, owned the *Freedom*, Hawkworth
House, numerous businesses, and it was all a
sham!

'Hawk,' she began slowly. 'You know that, for
all our difficulties this last year, that if ever I

were in trouble and needed help I would come to you, don't you?' She looked at him frowningly.

His eyes were narrowed. 'I would certainly hope so,' he nodded.

'And that if you were—troubled, about anything, I would want to help you in any way I can?' She watched him closely.

He gave an inclination of his head. 'I'm sure that you would.'

She moistened her lips at his unforthcoming answers. 'And—are you?' she prompted.

'Troubled?' he repeated in an amused voice. 'I can't think of anything offhand.'

He couldn't think of anything? He *couldn't* have changed this much!

'I may as well clean out your desk while I'm at the office.' He looked at her challengingly.

Whitney swallowed hard, knowing he expected her to continue to argue as to the fairness of her dismissal from the *National*. But the job that had come to mean so much to her the last year, since it had been the only thing she had in her life, no longer seemed important compared to the enormity of what Hawk was contemplating doing.

She shrugged. 'It's your newspaper.'

His eyes narrowed at her lack of protest. 'It's for the best, Whitney.'

'I'm sure it is,' she nodded.

His frown increased. 'Are you sure you're just over-tired? You don't seem quite yourself.'

A ghost of a smile curved her lips. 'Because I'm not losing my temper as I usually do?'

'Yes,' Hawk answered with complete honesty.

Her splutter of laughter was completely spontaneous; she hardly felt in the mood for laughter! 'No one could ever accuse you of charming me with compliments,' she derided ruefully.

'*That* wouldn't be in the least like me,' he said drily.

No, Hawk had never been accused of being an overly charming man, but women had always liked him nonetheless, although Hawk had never returned their obvious interest. Because of Geraldine.

'Hawk,'—she looked at him eagerly—'couldn't your business wait a few days? We could have fun together if we left now, like we used to.' Geraldine was seasick as soon as she stepped on board *Freedom*, and so the two of them had always been alone on their trips, since one memorable trip when Geraldine had spent several days confined to her suite claiming she was about to die if she didn't get off. Whitney had felt sorry for her, but she had also been grateful for the times alone with Hawk.

His golden eyes were hooded by heavy lids as he shook his head regretfully. 'My business can't wait.'

He made the statement with such finality that Whitney knew it couldn't. Were things that desperate, then?

'Rest today, Whitney,' he said gently at her disappointed expression. 'And then this evening we'll do something together, I promise.'

Whitney didn't like his cajoling tone at all.

'Tell me something, Hawk,' she snapped. 'When you kissed me yesterday, did I seem like a child to you?'

His mouth tightened, the skin taut across his high cheekbones. 'You know you didn't——'

'Then don't try to placate me as if I still am one!' She glared at him. 'I'm twenty-two, and I don't need the promise of a "treat" to make up for a disappointment like I did when I was fifteen!'

Hawk was breathing raggedly as he looked at her with exasperation. 'I was only——'

'I know what you "were only",' she cut in heatedly, standing up to cover the distance between them with determined strides. 'And if you're going to console me with a treat I'd rather have one of my own choosing!' Her arms curved up about his neck as she pulled his head down to her.

She was convinced Hawk had remained unmoved when he had kissed her yesterday, and she was equally convinced he wasn't going to stay that way today!

She put everything she had into that kiss, all her love, every ounce of experience she had gained with the few boys she had dated since leaving school, her lips parted against his, forcing him to meet the caress, moving erotically against him, feeling him stiffen as her tongue made a daring exploration of his mouth.

She groaned her satisfaction when his arms moved slowly about her waist, snuggling against him as she felt the leap of desire his body was too

aroused to deny. That physical show of his desire
was all that she needed to spur her on to deepen
the caress, moaning low in her throat as Hawk
became the master.

She had known he had to be a sensual man,
and the intense passion of his kiss told her that
she had been right in the assumption, his hands
moving restlessly up and down her spine.
Whitney wanted those hands on her breasts.

'What do you think you're doing?' Hawk
demanded dazedly, snatching his hands away
from where she had nuzzled her breasts against
him. He stepped back, his expression stunned.
'What the hell do you think you're doing?' he
said again, this time with harsh disbelief.

She held her head high. 'I can't believe you
don't know,' she bit out.

'Whitney . . .?' He looked totally bewildered,
by her actions as well as his own. 'That wasn't
funny,' he finally grated.

Her harsh laugh lacked amusement. 'It wasn't
meant to be!'

His mouth thinned. 'If it was supposed to show
me you're grown up, I already knew that!'

She could have cried with the frustration of her
misunderstood motives. But why should she have
thought the kiss she had forced on him should
have made him see her as other than Whitney
Morgan, the daughter of the man who had been
his best friend, the child he had agreed to care
for. That agreement had cost him so much: the
career he loved, the wife he was obsessed with,
and now the money that had been all he had left.

It was proof of Hawk's generosity that he didn't actually hate her.

She turned away. 'I'm sorry. I—I was angry, and——Well, you know me, Hawk,' she dismissed brittlely. 'I do stupid things when I'm angry. How is your shin today?' she queried lightly.

'Bruised,'—his mouth twisted—'but I'll live.' He looked at his wristwatch, seeming relieved that she had dismissed the significance of the kiss they had just shared. 'I really do have to go now.' He frowned. 'Are you going to be all right here on your own all day?'

'You mean, am I going to try and escape?' she derided tauntingly.

'You aren't a prisoner!' Hawk rasped. 'God, Whitney, will it be such a punishment having to spend a little time with me?'

It could have been wonderful, if she hadn't known that during the next few days Hawk was probably going to take a step that would ruin his life! 'You aren't going to be here most of the time,' she reminded him distractedly, her eyes suddenly taking on a glow. 'I know, why don't you let me come with you?' she suggested excitedly.

'It's a business meeting——'

'I wouldn't get in the way,' she hastened to assure him. 'You wouldn't even know I was there.'

'Whitney,' he reasoned slowly. 'You just said you were tired.'

'I am,' she nodded. 'But I'll never sleep, you know I never can during the day.'

'You could still rest.'

She was losing this argument, she could tell. And yet it had seemed like such a good idea; if she was with him he could hardly meet or talk to Tom Beresford! 'You just don't want me around,' she pouted, watching him from beneath the fan of her lowered lashes. He was actually smiling!

'I remember the last time you sent me on that guilt trip,' he mused. 'I ended up taking you to Wimbledon every day for two weeks to watch the tennis, and I hate the sport!'

'You told me you enjoyed it,' she recalled indignantly.

'I didn't want to hurt your feelings,' he grinned. 'But this time I have to,' he stated. 'My meeting will be purely business; you would be bored out of your mind. No, Whitney,' he added firmly as she would have argued again. 'I've finally learnt how to say that to you,' he said self-derisively.

'You make me sound like a spoilt brat,' she frowned.

'I only completed the job your father had already started,' he teased, seeing her indignation.

'Except that I'm not your daughter,' she pointed out huskily.

His expression hardened. 'You are the daughter I would have wished for if I'd had one.'

Whitney felt thoroughly deflated once he had left. A *daughter*! That couldn't possibly be how Hawk thought of her!

*　　　*　　　*

She took advantage of Hawk's absence to take out the file and photographs on Tom Beresford and spread them out on the desk in the library; no one else on board was aware of the significance of them being in her possession. No matter how many times she went through it all she couldn't see anything in it which Hawk could use to barter with Tom Beresford. Oh, she had done her research on the man thoroughly, had taken dozens of photographs, but she hadn't yet been able to find evidence of actual payments being made. Hawk was going to be very disappointed when he did eventually take possession of them. And she had no doubt that he would; she couldn't continue to lie about them indefinitely.

But he made no mention of either the file or the photographs that evening when he handed her the other things from her desk. He looked more strained than ever, though, and she desperately wished there were some way she could help him. But he had made it more than clear he didn't want her interference.

Sleep didn't prove as elusive that night, the lengthy bath she had taken before retiring relaxing her, Hawk having retreated to the library straight after dinner, claiming he had work to do. Whitney didn't know if he had work to do or if he was just avoiding being alone with her. The bath was welcome, anyway, and she fell asleep shortly after climbing between the silk sheets.

Quite what woke her up again she didn't know, but she woke with a start, sitting straight up in bed. The bedside clock illuminated one o'clock.

The same time Glyn Briant had come on board
the previous night! It couldn't just be a
coincidence.

She pulled on her masculine bathrobe over the
practical silky nightshirt, quietly padding up on
deck. It was a beautifully clear night, very quiet
in this London marina, the air warm and light.

'What are you doing up here?' Hawk rasped
from the darkness.

She turned with a guilty start, relief shooting
through her when she saw he was alone, having
come from the direction of the sun-deck at the
back of the yacht, still wearing the cream shirt
and brown trousers he had worn at dinner earlier,
although the shirt was now unbuttoned at the
collar and the suit jacket had been discarded. He
looked beautiful!

'Something woke me,' she shrugged, turning
sharply as she heard the purr of a car engine on
the dock. She saw the arc of the car headlights
before the car turned and only the tail-lights were
visible until it disappeared completely. She
turned back to Hawk with raised brows. 'A
visitor?' she asked with feigned casualness.

He shrugged dismissively, although his gaze
didn't quite reach hers. 'Must have been to one of
the other yachts,' he disclaimed.

She didn't believe him, not after Glyn Briant's
nocturnal visit the night before. 'That must have
been what woke me,' she frowned. 'Haven't you
been to bed yet?' She *knew* he hadn't!

'I had some things to do before I retired.' He
eyed her warily.

'I see,' she nodded, making no effort to return to her own bed.

Golden eyes narrowed at this reluctance to leave. 'It's late, Whitney,' he snapped.

'Or early,' she acknowledged lightly. 'It depends on your point of view.'

He gave an impatient sigh. 'Aren't you sleepy?'

'Not particularly,' she shrugged.

'Well I am,' he said pointedly.

'I thought you had some things to do.' She looked up at him guilelessly.

'I've finished them,' he bit out, obviously very on edge.

'Then we may as well have a nightcap together,' she decided brightly.

'Whitney——'

'In the lounge or out on deck?' she asked, bulldozing over his objections. If she could just get him to *talk* to her. And the early hours of the morning were reputed to be good for that, the darkness of night seeming to loosen the tongue. Although she wasn't sure that would be true of Hawk!

'I already have a bottle of brandy out on deck,' he admitted reluctantly.

Whitney followed him to the lounge area at the back of the yacht, noting that *two* of the glasses on the tray had already been used. Glyn Briant had been here again tonight, she was sure of it.

'Thanks.' She smiled straight into Hawk's eyes as he handed her the brandy, curled up comfortably in one of the cushioned armchairs.

Hawk remained standing, his expression grim

as he sipped at his own drink; far from his second by the level of the brandy left in the decanter!

She drew in a deep breath. 'Is there anything I can do to help you?'

'Sorry?' He frowned darkly at the question.

Her shrug was deliberately casual. 'Well, I can never remember your being so busy you had to stay up half the night working.' Her expression was bland. God, how could she get him to talk to her! She couldn't just ask him outright if he was involved with Tom Beresford, that would just be asking for one of his chilly rebuffs. She had never felt so utterly helpless.

He shrugged. 'I told you I had things to do before we could leave.'

Whitney gave him a sharp look. 'The trip is still on, then?'

His eyes narrowed. 'Did I ever give the impression it wasn't?' he grated.

He hadn't said as much, but it was the assumption she had made, and she was sure that until a few minutes ago it had been a correct one. What had Glyn Briant told Hawk this evening to change those plans? Because for some reason the two men had now decided the trip was a good idea. Damn! She wished she had woken up earlier and had a chance to listen in on the conversation.

She gave a dismissive shrug. 'I presumed the next couple of days here were instead of a cruise.'

Hawk looked irritated. 'Two days won't do it.'

'How did Martin take the news of my dismissal?' She grimaced.

'No one questions my decision,' he told her

arrogantly. 'At least,' he added ruefully, 'almost no one.' He looked at her pointedly.

Whitney smiled. 'Martin wasn't too upset about losing his star reporter, then?'

Hawk turned away, his eyes narrowed as he gazed out at the other yachts moored about them. 'Not too upset, no,' he finally grated. 'I'll help you get another job once this is all over, Whitney,' he added harshly. 'If only you hadn't——'

'Yes?' she prompted, standing very close to his side, looking up at him with trusting eyes. She had to trust him eventually to do what was right and not what was easiest. 'Hawk——'

'Don't touch me!' He stepped back from her hand on his arm, his face rigid with disapproval as he swallowed some more of the brandy.

'Hawk . . .?' Her eyes reflected her hurt bewilderment at this complete physical rejection of her. He had never reacted in quite this way before.

His expression was grim. 'It's late, I've drunk too much brandy tonight, and I don't remember the last time I had a woman. I'm too damned vulnerable right now, Whitney!' he angrily admitted.

Her eyes widened, all the signs of physical arousal there for her to see now that she knew to look for them. His eyes were glazed—and not just from the brandy—his face pale, muscle spasms in his jaw, his whole body rigid with physical tension. Hawk didn't need to admit to his weakness, it was all too apparent. Would he confide in her if they became lovers?

'Hawk——'

'Whitney, no!' He stepped back as she would have touched him again. 'I don't want you!'

'But you do,' she murmured confidently, feeling his heart leap beneath her hand as she placed it on his chest. 'Hawk, I'm here if you want me,' she encouraged throatily.

'I don't!' He shook his head, breathing rapidly.

'Hawk, it will be all right. I'm not a child, and we could give each other so much.'

'No!'

He didn't mean it, she could see that he didn't, only realising how much of her legs were laid bare as she followed his heated gaze down her body. 'Yes,' she insisted, moving determinedly towards him.

'I'd only be using you,' he groaned as she leant her body into his.

'Then use me, Hawk,' she encouraged huskily.

He swallowed convulsively. 'I can't.'

'You can.' She slowly unbuttoned his shirt.

'*We* can't.' He shook his head in desperation.

'*I* can.' She slipped his shirt off his shoulders.

She had seen him dressed in only a pair of bathing trunks hundreds of times, and yet there was something so much more primitively fascinating about seeing his bare chest bathed by moonlight, his trousers fitted low on his waist. The hair on his chest gleamed golden, and her fingers ached to know him.

'This is wrong, Whitney,' Hawk groaned as she placed featherlight kisses across his chest. 'Whitney, I can't stand it when you do that!' he groaned achingly as her tongue caressed the hard brown nubs on his chest. 'If you don't stop now . . .!'

She had no intention of stopping. The cloak of darkness had given her the courage to do all the things to him she had always longed to do, her hands caressing him as her lips slowly moved down his body. He made no further effort to resist her but neither did he encourage her, seeming lost to the explosive demands of his body.

Passivity could be as encouraging as a passionate response to a woman who had loved for as long as Whitney had, she felt, taking her fill of him as they lay down together on the sofa behind them.

They kissed heatedly, deeply, Hawk the master now as he lay half across her, impatiently pushing aside the robe to pull open the buttons of her nightshirt. So much for her not to show herself on deck; she was almost naked!

Her breasts fitted perfectly into the cup of his hands, as if both had been made for just such a purpose, and all the breath fled her body as he tugged the aching nipple into the moist warmth of his mouth.

Hawk, her arrogant Hawk, shuddered against her with need as her hand moved to caress his thigh, a groan of satisfaction escaping his lips as she claimed him.

He had a magnificent body, strong and yet gentle, and she wanted all of him, all he had to give.

Her mouth clung to his as she released her
arms from the robe and nightshirt, the two laying
discarded beneath her as she wrapped her naked
body about Hawk's. A spasm shot through his
body as her heated flesh moulded with his, her
nipples aching nubs that soon knew the pleasur-
able release of his lips and hands, their bodies
moist with perspiration as they clung together
amid the maelstrom.

Whitney had dreamed of this moment all of her
adult life, meeting all of the passionate demand
she had known Hawk was capable of with her
own need, rapidly reaching the point where she
needed him inside her, wanting to reach that fiery
haven with him.

She was on fire, so deliciously moist, welcoming
his lips and hands wherever they touched, her
thighs closing about him as he slowly caressed
her, her head falling back against his arm as the
warmth threatened to burst and engulf her.

Hawk tasted of brandy as his mouth parted
hers once again, but the two of them were
intoxicated with something so much more heady
than mere alcohol, Hawk's thighs moving against
her in rhythmic need now, the caress of his hand
matching that rhythm.

'Hawk!' she cried out as she knew she was
about to reach that haven without him, determined not to.

'You're going to hate me afterwards,' he
groaned, his tongue outlining her lips.

'As long as you know it's me I don't care,' she
assured him, knowing by the way he became so

suddenly still that it had been completely the wrong thing to say. She could have cried with her disappointment as Hawk looked down at her with dazed eyes, seeming to see her for the first time.

She had said she didn't mind if he used her, but she hadn't realised she would only be a substitute for the wife that had left him and that he still loved!

The robe was cool against her still-heated flesh as she struggled into it, bundling her nightshirt up in her hand as she watched Hawk cross the deck. He stood with his back towards her, his shoulders hunched over, his breathing ragged.

'We'll be having guests on board tomorrow,' he announced suddenly.

Her eyes widened; this certainly hadn't been what she had been expecting him to say!

He turned abruptly, the golden eyes tormented. 'Geraldine and her husband will be here for dinner.'

Now she realised why he had been drinking.

God! Could his visitor tonight have been Geraldine herself? Had the other woman left him aching and unassuaged?

With a cry of pain she turned and fled to the lower deck.

CHAPTER FIVE

HAWK wasn't on board the *Freedom* when Whitney finally left her suite the next morning, Stephen Hollister informing her that his employer had left hours ago to go to his office in town.

Maybe she had deserved the pain and humiliation Hawk had dealt her last night—after all he had told her he would only be using her—but he hadn't needed to be quite as cruel as he had been. A simple, 'I'm still in love with my ex-wife', would have done it; he hadn't needed to show her quite so eloquently that it had been Geraldine he had been thinking of as he made love to her.

Whitney couldn't help wondering if the other woman had been the driver of the car she had seen leaving. If Hawk were having an affair with the other woman while trying to do business with her second husband, Whitney couldn't help thinking he was in serious trouble, worse than she had even guessed. Tom Beresford would *never* sit back and accept Hawk having an affair with Geraldine.

Maybe she was being a little premature. Hawk had frankly admitted it had been some time since he made love to a woman, any woman, and his instantaneous response had been evidence of that.

But last night he had shown her that if he

couldn't have Geraldine, or a woman he could
pretend was Geraldine, then he didn't want a
woman at all. And Whitney knew she couldn't
stay on *Freedom* and see him again knowing that.

Getting off via the gangway proved to be
impossible, several of the crew always working or
talking there. And Whitney didn't think that was
accidental either; Hawk was taking no chances on
her getting away!

The only alternative seemed to be to go over
the side with it's drop into the water. If she
climbed over and then slowly lowered herself
there shouldn't be too much of a splash to alert
the crew to her movements when she let go.

The opportunity came after lunch, with several
of the crew downstairs having their own meal,
and the others relaxed as they chatted together
near the gangway. Whitney seized her chance.

She had never realised how high the sides of
the yacht were before!

It was almost her length again to the murky
water, and she knew that far from gliding into the
water as she had hoped to do she was going to
make quite a splash! Tears flowed unheeded
down her cheeks as she realised the ridiculous
situation she had got herself into now; she neither
had the strength to climb back up nor the nerve
to let go.

She was beginning to think her arms were
going to be wrenched out of their sockets when
someone swore directly above her. She looked up
guiltily to see Hawk glaring down at her.

He didn't say a word as he clasped hold of her

wrists and began to pull her back up on to the deck, but the grimness of his expression was speech enough; he was furiously angry.

Whitney used her feet to help herself up, soon standing next to him on the deck, her shoulders aching unbearably where they had taken the strain of her full weight the last half an hour.

'You little idiot!' Hawk rasped between gritted teeth as she rubbed the painful joints.

She shot him a scathing look. 'I already realise that, thank you,' she told him haughtily.

'Just what were you hoping to achieve?' he demanded to know.

'Freedom!' She glared at him.

'You don't even swim all that well; you could have drowned! I thought I was seeing things when I went down to my suite to change and saw you dangling outside the window!' He still looked a little shaken.

She had even been stupid enough to choose Hawk's suite window to climb past! Although she knew she couldn't have held on much longer, and then there would have been even more of a fuss, with the crew knowing of her stupidity, too.

'How long had you been there?' Hawk frowned, taking over the task of massaging her sore shoulders, his movements unconsciously arousing.

'Too long,' she groaned.

'Why, Whitney?' He was suddenly still. 'If it's about last night——'

'Last night is only part of it,' she cut in

sharply. 'I don't like what you're doing, Hawk.'

'Am I hurting you?' His hands rested lightly on her shoulders as he frowned his concern.

'I don't mean this.' She shrugged away from his touch. 'Why are you involved with Geraldine and Tom Beresford?'

He avoided her gaze, his expression shuttered. 'That's none of your business,' he rasped.

'You're destroying yourself——'

'I'm doing what I have to do,' he bit out coldly.

She shook her head. 'Well I don't have to be a party to it.'

'You're already too deeply involved to get out now without getting hurt,' he told her grimly.

Did he know she was in love with him? She avidly searched the harsh remoteness of his face, realising he was talking about her knowledge of Tom Beresford and not what had happened between the two of them last night.

'Can't you see that this isn't the way to get Geraldine back?' she groaned.

He stiffened. 'Why should I let her go if I want her back?'

'It wasn't your decision!'

'Whitney——' He stopped, his mouth compressed angrily. 'Give me the file and photographs you have on Tom Beresford and maybe, just maybe, I'll be able to keep you out of it.'

She frowned. 'You know I have them?'

He nodded abruptly. 'They're probably wrapped up inside that plastic bag with your handbag.' He looked pointedly at the bundle she held on to so tightly. 'Right this very minute,' he added grimly.

She blushed her guilt. 'If you knew that all the time,'—and she knew that he had—'why didn't you just take them?'

He shrugged. 'I wanted you to give them to me without coercion.'

'But there's nothing in there for him to worry about,' she protested. 'Only supposition and conjecture. Tom Beresford is too clever to incriminate himself,' she added disgustedly.

'Let me see.' Hawk put out his hand for them.

She fought a battle within herself, all the time knowing that if she didn't give them to Hawk he could just take them by force, that the time for being patient was long past. And although she had done her research well, had enough to confirm her own suspicions, she really couldn't think why Tom Beresford wanted them so desperately; she had gone through both the file and photographs again closely that morning and found nothing to really worry Tom Beresford. Except the fact that she was interested enough to have taken the photographs and collected the information. To a man in Tom Beresford's position that could be enough to make him nervous.

With a sigh she took the file and the envelope containing the photographs out of her polythene-wrapped bag and gave them to Hawk, frowning as he moved to the low coffee-table to tip the contents out on to the surface.

Hundreds of instant snapshots fell out of the

envelope, Tom Beresford on his own, meeting people, with Geraldine, Geraldine on her own, Geraldine meeting people. The last had just been a morbid curiosity about the woman Hawk loved.

Hawk looked up at her ruefully. 'If nothing else, Tom should be able to have you charged with invasion of privacy,' he drawled mockingly, beginning to sort through the numerous photographs.

'He would have too many explanations to make if he did that,' she said disgustedly.

He shrugged. 'You aren't a bad photographer.' He spoke absently, lingering over some of the photographs and quickly flicking through others.

Whitney watched him curiously. 'What are you looking for?'

His expression instantly became guarded. 'You don't have too much concrete evidence on Tom Beresford,' he challenged, instead of answering her. 'You told Martin you were close to accusing him.'

Her cheeks became flushed with anger. 'I've got enough to have him worried.'

'Maybe,' Hawk acknowledged non-committally, collecting all the information together. 'I thought you would have a lot more than this after six months.'

'You're going to just hand all that over to him?' she realised wearily.

'They needn't concern you any more,' he told her harshly.

'And you,' she groaned. 'Aren't I to be concerned about you, either?'

He shrugged. 'You were trying to leave just now, and now that you've given me the information I needed I'll see what I can do about having you taken off *Freedom*.'

'Ask his permission, you mean,' she scorned. 'Hawk——'

'Whitney!' he grated, standing up, his superior height forbidding. 'For God's sake just stay out of it now. Later——Well, maybe later we can talk.'

'When?' she groaned heavily. 'When you've become as corrupt as he is?'

His head went back coldly. 'I think you should go and have a soak in the bath; your shoulders will begin to stiffen up otherwise.'

It was a dismissal, and one she was loath to obey. 'Why should you want to be associated with Tom Beresford when he's married to Geraldine?' she persisted. 'You should hate the man.'

'Or pity him!' Hawk rasped.

She shook her head in bewilderment. 'I don't understand you.'

'You don't need to,' he bit out. 'In fact, it's better if you don't. I was responsible for keeping you safe for six years of your life, and I don't want anything to happen to you now.'

'As you said before, I'm already involved,' she derided. 'And no matter what you would like to think about last night you responded to *me*,' she challenged, needing that reassurance at least if she were to remain here with him. Trying to get off *Freedom* had been a mistake, she realised that now; she could be no help to Hawk if she didn't stay with him.

He drew in a shuddering breath. 'I know exactly what happened last night, but do you?'

She couldn't meet his gaze. 'I know you're worth so much more than Geraldine Beresford!'

'Don't attempt anything tonight, Whitney,' he urged coldly. 'You could ruin everything.'

'I wish I could!'

'Don't, Whitney.' He grasped her arms and shook her slightly. 'There's too much at stake for this.'

Tears flooded her eyes. 'If it's money——'

'It isn't,' he refuted grimly.

She drew in a ragged breath as he took away the excuse she had been using for his behaviour. 'Then why?' she groaned.

He shook his head, releasing her abruptly, thrusting his hands into his trouser pockets. 'Go and take your bath. And for God's sake behave yourself tonight.'

'And if I don't?'

Hawk sighed. 'Then we could both have reason to regret it!'

Maybe it was because in the past Hawk had always seemed so strong and confident to her that she found his weakness now so upsetting. Whatever it was she felt thoroughly dejected as she got ready for what promised to be a tension-filled evening, at best—at worst, a disaster!

But if Geraldine thought she could treat her with that cool condescension she had usually shown her in the past she was going to be disappointed; Whitney was no longer that slightly insecure teenager who flinched at every cutting barb; she was a woman now, and she wasn't afraid to show that she wanted Hawk for herself.

Whitney doubted Hawk had taken note of the lack of actual material to the shimmering purple and black gown when he had thrown it into her case yesterday, and if he had he probably wouldn't have realised how the material clung to and enhanced the curves of her body, narrow straps over her shoulders that widened only slightly over her breasts, so that a considerable amount of their creamy softness was still visible at the sides, her nipples firmly erect against the gossamer material. To emphasise the lack of material at the top of the dress she had swept her hair loosely on top of her head, the back of the dress dipping almost to the base of her spine.

She felt beautifully confident in the dress, her head held high as she left her cabin to join Hawk in the lounge, faltering only slightly as she saw Glyn Briant was already there.

She moved forward determinedly as the two men broke off their conversation as soon as she entered the room, her gaze fixed challengingly on Glyn Briant as she crossed the carpeted floor to join them. He was a man of about Hawk's age, with short brown hair, and brown eyes that were coolly assessing at the moment. He was good-looking in a pleasant sort of way, seeming to become visibly less obtrusive as he sensed her hostility towards him.

'Miss Morgan,' he greeted smoothly, putting out his hand.

'Mr Briant.' She ignored his hand, bristling

even more when he smilingly let it fall back to his side. 'All alone this evening?' she taunted.

He gave an inclination of his head. 'My employer and his wife will be here soon.'

'You were given the job of coming on ahead to "check us out",' she derided.

'Whitney——'

'Could you be dangerous, Miss Morgan?' Glyn Briant watched her with narrowed eyes.

She flicked a glance at Hawk, whatever reaction he had first shown to the seductive style of her gown erased by the tension about his mouth and eyes. He didn't seem at all in awe of the other man, just displeased with the way she was baiting him. 'Perhaps Hawk could better answer that?' she challenged softly.

'I gave up trying to second-guess you years ago, Whitney,' he said wearily. 'You'll go right ahead and do what you want, regardless.'

Regardless of what? If there really were a danger to Hawk because of her reckless behaviour then she would stop it right now, couldn't bear it if anything happened to him, no matter what he was involved in.

She put her arm through the crook of his, smiling at Glyn Briant, although the warmth didn't erase the pain from her eyes. 'Hawk exaggerates,' she dismissed. 'He's always been able to make me do exactly what he wants.'

A speculative gleam entered the narrowed brown eyes. 'Really?'

'No,' Hawk rasped harshly.

'I'm sure the lady knows best, Hawk,' the other man drawled.

'The *lady* is still very much a child—despite
the dress.' He frowned at her darkly. 'Did I pack
that for you?' he demanded.

Her eyes were widely innocent. 'What's wrong?
Don't you like it?'

'A man would have to be blind and senile not
to, Miss Morgan,' Glyn Briant mocked.

'Well I know he isn't blind,' she drawled.

'Well, Hawk?' the other man challenged
laughingly at his stony silence.

He drew in a ragged breath. 'I'm beginning to
wonder myself about the senility,' he grated.

'But, Hawk, you know I——'

'Whitney!' he silenced forcefully.

'He's too modest, Mr Briant,' she confided
lightly. 'And I'm too much of a lady to tell.'

'Hell!' Hawk swung away from her, glaring at
the other man. 'I can't go through with this,' he
told him firmly.

'Hawk——'

'I was her guardian for six years, damn it, and
now she thinks I'm some sort of criminal!' Hawk
was breathing hard.

Whitney blinked dazedly at his vehemence, and
Glyn Briant looked furious at the outburst.

'Hawk, we agreed——'

'*You* agreed,' he snapped. 'And I went along
with it because I thought you knew what you
were doing. But she'll ruin everything if we don't
tell her the truth, can't you see that? She tried to
go over the side of the yacht earlier today just to
get away from me and she doesn't even swim that
well! And don't try and tell me you have to OK

this with some damned superior,' he bit out
furiously. 'I have to tell her *now*!'

Glyn Briant looked even more angry than
Hawk. 'It's too dangerous!'

'The little she knows is too dangerous!'

'Hawk——'

'Either you tell her, Glyn, or I do,' Hawk told
him coldly.

Whitney was utterly bewildered. *What* did
Hawk want her to know?

The other man still looked furious. 'I'm not
going to jeopardise years of work!'

'You—or me, Glyn,' Hawk repeated threa-
teningly.

'If he gets away after all this time——'

'He won't,' Hawk promised harshly. 'But
you'll just have to accept that I value Whitney's
respect as much as you want him!'

'Damn you!' Glyn groaned.

'Yes,' Hawk acknowledged heavily.

'I'll tell her only as much as she needs to know
to exonerate you,' the other man finally conceded
harshly. 'But no more than that,' he warned
coldly.

Hawk looked straight at Whitney's puzzled
face before nodding slowly.

Whitney turned to Glyn Briant questioningly.
She still felt afraid for Hawk, and yet now she felt
anticipation too; exoneration had to mean he
wasn't guilty of anything!

Glyn Briant's mouth tightened as the sound of
a car arriving could be heard outside. 'That's
them now,' he rasped impatiently. 'All you need

to know, Whitney, is that I'm an undercover policeman and Hawk is helping me with my inquiries.'

All the colour drained out of her face, her eyes deep violet pools of fear. 'Hawk . . .?'

'Well done, Glyn.' He glared at the other man before taking Whitney in his arms. 'You've just succeeded in convincing her you're about to arrest me!'

'Believe me,'—the other man strode purposefully to the door—'at the moment that doesn't sound such a bad idea! Oh, for God's sake,' he bit out impatiently. 'Hawk is helping me to make an arrest,' he snapped. 'He isn't guilty of anything, has never been guilty of anything. Satisfied?' he grated to Hawk.

'Whitney?' he frowned down at her anxiously.

Relief brightened her eyes as she swayed weakly against him.

CHAPTER SIX

AFTER what she had been imagining the last two days the relief at learning that it had all been a mistake, that Hawk was out to trap Tom Beresford, too, was immense.

'Why didn't you tell me?' She looked up at him with accusing eyes once the relief faded to be replaced by anger.

He grimaced. 'You heard Glyn, he wouldn't have told you now if I hadn't pressured him into it. But I've seen the look in your eyes since I told you Tom Beresford is coming on board tonight, and after years of being responsible for you I just couldn't stand the thought of you believing I'm guilty of something,' he rasped. 'Maybe I was wrong, maybe it was better when you didn't know the truth,' he muttered. 'My self-gratification isn't going to mean a whole lot if we lose him now!'

'But——'

'Just behave yourself tonight, Whitney,' he bit out. 'And I'll try to explain more later. Just don't let me down,' he warned at the sound of approaching voices.

She would have lain down and let him use her as a carpet if he had asked her to now that her faith in him had been restored. But she knew he would never ask her to, knew that he would never ask anything of her, that he only felt *responsible* for her. God, how that cut to the quick.

But her hurt confusion over his actions had gone now, and she was standing proudly at his side when Tom Beresford, Geraldine and Alex Cordell entered the lounge, closely followed by Glyn Briant.

Tom Beresford's eyes narrowed on her speculatively, but it was to Geraldine her gaze strayed— and remained. The other woman was more beautiful than ever, her red hair a gleaming cap of riotous curls that framed the gamine beauty of her face with its dominating green eyes with their cat-like slant, the perfection of her curvaceous figure clearly shown in the clinging red gown that enriched the colour of her hair rather than detracted from it. As she stood next to her husband, her diminutive size seemed to make him look taller and more muscular, although Whitney knew that if she were to stand next to him she would still manage to make him look small, once again having three-inch heels on her sandals. The other woman's ability to look small and helpless had always made her feel big and clumsy!

But if she had been looking for changes in Geraldine, the other woman had been using the same time to assess her—and by the angry flash in her eyes she didn't like what she was seeing.

'Hawk.' Tom Beresford took the other man's hand in a firm grip. 'And Miss Morgan,' he added smoothly. 'I had no idea we would meet again so soon.'

She felt Hawk stiffen at her side, and bit back the cutting retort she had been about to make. 'I never can resist Hawk when he asks me for something,' she returned huskily, hoping her double meaning would be lost on no one.

Silver brows rose speculatively. 'Really?' Tom Beresford said questioningly.

She gave a bright smile. 'When he asked me to be his hostess tonight I just couldn't refuse,' she explained lightly. 'Hello, Geraldine, it's good to see you again,' she greeted softly.

The other woman gave a mocking inclination of her head. 'You always were half in love with Hawk,' she taunted disparagingly.

Colour darkened her cheeks. But she knew the other woman had hoped to disconcert her, and she wouldn't give her that satisfaction. 'Only half?' she challenged.

Anger flared in the narrowed green eyes. 'We often laughed together over your childish infatuation for him,' Geraldine bit out waspishly.

Whitney didn't for a moment believe Hawk would laugh at her in such a cruel way, but just the thought of him knowing she had always loved him and that he had been embarrased by it was enough to make her pale. There was no way she could turn and look at him—as she longed to do. 'He doesn't appear to be laughing now,' she returned confidently.

'You——'

'Should you really be showing this much interest in your ex-husband's love life, Geraldine?' she derided at the other woman's outburst, knowing she had hit a nerve as Geraldine flushed angrily.

'Ladies,' Tom Beresford lightly chided, although the coldness remained in his pale blue eyes. 'You made your choice, Geraldine—and it would seem Hawk has made his,' he added harshly. 'I like your taste in women, Hawkworth,' he rasped.

Hawk gave an acknowledging inclination of his head. 'Alex.' He put out his hand to the third man in the room, Tom Beresford's other quietly watchful 'minder'. 'I expected to see you earlier.'

'Glyn got that job,' the man returned in the reserved manner that seemed to be typical of him. 'Nice craft.'

'I think so,' Hawk nodded.

'I'm starting to feel ill already.' Geraldine's caustic tone put a dampener on the conversation, her gaze critical as she looked around the refurbished lounge. 'I really must give you the name of our interior designer, Hawk,' she dismissed scathingly, sitting down.

'I think this room is perfect as it is.' Whitney couldn't stop herself leaping to Hawk's defence.

Green eyes swept over her derisively. 'But then our tastes have always been so—different,' Geraldine finally drawled.

Whitney could feel her anger rising, knowing this last had been a slight to Hawk. Her snapped retort froze in her throat as she felt his arm move possessively about her waist.

She didn't know how he could just stand by and let Geraldine insult him in this way!

Probably the same way he always had, because he loved her. And with that realisation came another one. Hawk could be helping Glyn Briant to catch Tom Beresford because, once he had, Geraldine would be free again! Whitney's relief at knowing he wasn't guilty of anything turned to dismay as she realised his motive.

'But not necessarily better,' she bit out resentfully, moving away from Hawk as she did so. 'Hawk, perhaps our guests would like a drink?' she prompted, in need of a sustaining drink herself.

The conversation certainly couldn't be said to be flowing smoothly as they waited for dinner to be served, Tom Beresford only speaking occasionally, as did Hawk, the two 'minders' sitting quietly watchful at the back of the room, so it was left to Whitney and Geraldine to fill in the gaps— and as neither woman made any attempt to hide their dislike of the other the conversation was fraught with tension. It was no better during the meal either.

There were so many questions Whitney wanted to ask Hawk, so much he still had to tell her, that all this seemed a waste of time to her. Surely Hawk didn't actually have to socialise with the man to pretend to do business with him. Or was it Geraldine he really wanted to see? The thought made Whitney pale.

'Would you care for a stroll on deck, Miss Morgan?' Tom Beresford offered, his all-seeing gaze seeming to guess the reason for her sudden distress.

'No! Er—thank you,' she added abruptly at Hawk's sharp look.

'You're looking a little pale,' Hawk frowned.

She felt pale, had never felt so sick in her life, the food she had forced past her lips heavy on her stomach, the realisation that Hawk was probably doing all this so that he could have Geraldine back making her feel ill. She could almost have wished it *had* been because he needed the money badly enough to use any means to get it.

Tom Beresford stood up. 'I really must insist, Miss Morgan.' He came round the table to pull back her chair for her. 'You look as if you're about to pass out!'

Hawk's expression hardened. 'Whitney——'

'She'll be fine with me, Hawkworth,' the older man rasped.

Whitney was barely aware of Alex Cordell standing up to follow them quietly out on to the deck. It was another clear, moonlit night, and she breathed deeply of the clean air.

'Feeling better?' Tom Beresford asked not unkindly, his eyes warm.

'A little,' she lied. 'Should you have left your wife with Hawk?'

His mouth twisted. 'She hates him,' her husband stated flatly.

'*What?*'

He gave a mocking inclination of his head. ' "A woman scorned . . ." '

'Geraldine wasn't scorned,' she scoffed. 'Hawk loved her. Why, he——' She broke off as she realised what she had been about to do. Glyn Briant had been right to doubt her; she had almost blown his cover because of a jealousy that she should have accepted long ago. 'He did everything he could to make her happy,' she amended tightly.

'My wife is a very demanding woman.' Tom Beresford shrugged. 'And Hawk is a very demanding man. He asked Geraldine for one thing too many.'

'Her love!'

'Her fidelity,' Tom Beresford murmured, leaning on the rail to stare sightlessly across the water. 'My wife is something of an alley cat,' he added grimly.

'You know that and yet you——' She broke off, shaking her head. 'What is it about the woman that makes men love her?' she added disgustedly.

He gave a mirthless laugh. 'I can only answer for myself—who else did you have in mind?'

She swallowed hard at the sharpness of his gaze. Hawk was relying on her not to let him down, and to reveal that he was still in love with Geraldine would ruin everything for him, possibly even endanger his life. 'Hawk loved her once,' she said calmly. 'But not any more.'

Tom Beresford gave her a sideways glance. 'Not now he's in love with you, hmm?'

'That's right,' she challenged, knowing this man had to believe she and Hawk were lovers; it was the only acceptable explanation—to him—of her presence on board.

The man at her side nodded approvingly. 'And how is the story on me going?'

She stiffened indignantly, knowing he had to know she could never do that story now that Hawk was involved. 'Hawk has decided—he's decided that it wouldn't capture the public interest,' she rasped.

'I see,' he murmured softly.

'At the moment,' she couldn't resist adding defiantly, hating this man's look of triumph.

He turned to lean back against the rail, supremely self-confident. 'Maybe you should have consulted your lover before putting yourself to the trouble of doing all that research,' he drawled.

She glanced uncomfortably at Alex Cordell as he stood a short distance away from them. How could the man stand there and listen so impassively to this totally private conversation? No doubt he was paid very well to forget anything he overheard. Nevertheless, it was disconcerting having this conversation listened to so closely.

'He wasn't my lover then,' she snapped.

'Are you more faithful to him than Geraldine was?' he derided.

'I happen to love him—which is more than Geraldine ever did!' she scorned with distaste. 'Now if you'll excuse me I think I'll go back inside; the air out here isn't any cleaner after all!' She turned and walked away.

Tom Beresford caught hold of her arm, swinging her round to face him. 'I hope, for your sake,' he muttered fiercely, 'that Hawk can control you.'

Her eyes flashed. 'He——'

'Feeling better, Whitney?' Hawk spoke pleasantly out of the darkness.

She turned to glare at him. 'Not particularly, no!' She was breathing hard in her agitation.

Hawk smiled at the other man, ignoring Whitney's anger. 'Your wife is feeling decidedly seasick, Tom,' he drawled. 'She's talking about leaving.'

The other man's expression hardened. 'I'll go and talk to her,' he muttered.

Whitney breathed easier once he had left, taking Alex Cordell with him. 'How can you even *pretend* to do business with him?' she said shakily.

'For God's sake,' Hawk bit out, dragging her to the back of the yacht, away from the lounge and his guests. 'You've only been told that so you *don't* talk out of turn,' he grated, his eyes as hard as gold. 'Glyn wasn't joking when he said there's a lot at stake.'

Whitney frowned her agitation. 'Why doesn't he just arrest him?'

'He will,' Hawk nodded grimly.

'When?'

'When the time is right,' he told her forcefully. 'Now, are you going to rejoin them and behave yourself or shall I tell them you've gone to your cabin because you don't feel well?'

Behaving herself meant being polite to people she despised, and she had done enough of that for one evening. 'Can you do that?' she frowned.

His mouth twisted into a humourless smile. 'As long as you appear to be under my control I can do anything,' he rasped bitterly. 'Between you and Geraldine the two of you have managed to give the impression that you have been suffering from unrequited love for me for years!'

Colour darkened her cheeks. 'It was just the way the conversation flowed.'

'I know that,' he nodded wearily. 'Although it served its purpose; everyone is convinced that we're now lovers.'

'Even Geraldine?' she taunted, stung that it hadn't even occurred to him that it might actually be the truth.

'Couldn't you tell?' he derided.

'Aren't you afraid she might cause trouble for you?' she frowned.

'Geraldine has a lover of her own she wouldn't want Tom to know about,' he rasped.

Whitney looked at him searchingly in the gloom. Could *he* possibly be Geraldine's lover? She suddenly felt ill again. 'I think I will go down to my cabin.' She avoided Hawk's gaze now. 'Please make my excuses to your guests.'

'Whitney——'

'Good night, Hawk,' she cut in quickly, needing to be on her own.

She was shaking with relief when he let her go. She had felt so happy when Glyn Briant had told her of Hawk's part in his scheme to arrest Tom Beresford, but now it suddenly seemed worse than ever. She had thought Hawk accepted that Geraldine had gone out of his life after the divorce, but now it was obvious he would try to do anything to get her back. Her own love for Hawk seemed even more futile.

She was completely unprepared for Hawk's entrance to her suite after only the briefest of knocks two hours later!

She had showered and changed into lilac silk pyjamas, but she had continued to move restlessly about her lounge, feeling like a caged lion must do. Then a short time ago she had heard the murmur of voices out on deck, and presumed the guests were leaving.

'We have to talk.' Hawk shut the door firmly behind him. Having discarded his dinner jacket and left it somewhere, he removed his tie to unbutton the collar of his shirt. 'I'm getting sick and tired of you walking away from me in the middle of a conversation!' he flared.

She stiffened resentfully, having no idea how the movement thrust her pebble-hard nipples against her silk top. 'As far as I was concerned that particular conversation was over!'

His mouth thinned as he ran an impatient hand through the thickness of his hair. 'And as far as *I'm* concerned it's barely begun,' he grated. 'Every time Geraldine's name is mentioned you freeze up on me.'

'You know why,' Whitney glared at him.

'If I did maybe it wouldn't make me so damned angry,' he bit out tersely.

Whitney was past caring, totally disgusted with his method of getting Geraldine back. 'You're her lover——'

'Her *what*?' he demanded icily, his eyes wide with disbelief.

Whitney swallowed hard in the face of his anger. ' "She has a lover",' she mimicked. '*You're* Geraldine's lover,' she said again, challengingly.

Flames shot out of the golden eyes, Hawk's hands clenched into fists at his side. 'I'm no one's lover,' he finally grated, seeming to exert tremendous control to stop himself from shaking her until her teeth rattled.

'Why else would you be involved in this if it weren't for her?' Whitney scorned. 'Glyn Briant may think you're helping him but really you just want Geraldine back. And without her rich second husband she would instinctively turn to you. She already has!'

Hawk was very pale, his eyes appearing a deeper gold than ever, his body rigid with tension. 'You can't really believe that,' he bit out tautly.

'Of course I believe it. I wouldn't have said it otherwise,' she derided contemptuously.

Hawk drew in a ragged breath. 'Come here to me, Whitney, and we'll see who's lover I am!'

Her eyes were widely startled as she stared at him with apprehension. 'Hawk——'

'I said, come here, damn it!' he bit out, the fire in his eyes pulling her towards him even as she shook her head in protest. His mouth twisted tauntingly as she stood in front of him. 'With the experience you claim to have you should be able to tell I haven't had a woman in more months than I care to think about, let alone made love to my ex-wife!'

'Then why——'

'I'm not in the mood to answer any more accusations, Whitney,' he rasped, his arms drawing her in to him. 'I've taken all I'm going to from you the last few days!'

He intended to make love to her, she could see it in his eyes, and she swayed weakly against him. Even if she only had this one time with him to remember it would be better than the nothing she had lived with for so long.

But a last-minute thought made her hesitate, Hawk's eyes becoming as cold as ice. 'Hawk——'

'I know exactly who you are, Whitney,' he grated. 'It's time you learnt who *I* am.'

'But I know——'

'No,' he cut in slowly. 'I don't think you do! I'm a man, just a man, and I make mistakes just like other men. I laugh, I cry, I *feel*. It's time I came down off that pedestal you're so frightened I might be falling off,' he grated harshly.

She had never put him on a pedestal, she was all too aware of how mortal he was, but before she could tell him any of that his mouth had moved possessively over hers. Then she didn't want to talk any more, her body melting into his, her lids closing instinctively over smoky violet eyes.

Hawk dragged his mouth across her cheek and down the length of her throat, pushing aside the material there to search the silky hollows. Whitney's head fell back to allow him easy access to her heated skin, clinging to the broadness of his shoulders as rivulets of pleasure claimed her body.

His hands shook slightly as he released the buttons on the silk jacket. 'God, this is so damned sexy,' he groaned as the material dropped noiselessly to the floor. 'No other woman could have looked as sexy.' His hands moved over her restlessly from breast to thigh.

The fact that he had at last called her a woman didn't go unnoticed by Whitney. It was what she had always wanted, her eyes glowing as she met his gaze. 'You make me feel that way, Hawk,' she told him huskily. 'Only you.'

He didn't answer, intent on the rosy peaks pushed so eagerly against his mouth, releasing the single button on her pyjama trousers even as he took one fiery nub into his mouth, his hands firm on her hips as the trousers slid in a lilac pool at her feet.

The feel of his lips and tongue on her aching breasts was ecstasy.

Hawk's hands shook as he held her, his breath a ragged rasp, a flush of passion in his cheeks as he raised his head to fuse his mouth with hers once more, his hands instruments of torture now as his fingertips barely grazed the aching fullness of her breasts, almost sobbing her need for his deeper caresses as she leaned into him heavily.

'Oh God, please, Hawk,' she choked. 'Please!'

The bed felt soft against her back as he laid her down on the sheet, throwing his own clothes to the floor, his fiery gaze, flames flickering in the depths of his eyes, never leaving her flushed and wanting face.

Her body caught fire at the touch of Hawk's as he lay beside her, one hand cupping her cheek as he claimed her mouth. His body was lean and yet muscular, perfectly matched to hers as he moved restlessly above her.

His caresses had inflamed her, made her weak with longing, and yet as she felt his thighs probing against hers she knew she wasn't yet ready for this intrusion. But Hawk was in the throes of a desire he couldn't control, that drove him on to possession, his mouth on hers as he claimed her pain as his own, groaning low in his throat as he entered her completely, their bodies merged.

For a moment Whitney felt invaded rather than loved, sure she couldn't accommodate the strength of him. But her body had other ideas, accepting him, encouraging him, the sensual warmth making her taut with desire as she began to move beneath him.

As the rhythm became a crescendo, the fire in her body raging out of control, she clung to his shoulders as her support, desperate to reach that inferno that would claim them both into its depth. And then it was too late for her, Hawk gasping his own release, his body taut before he lay damply against her.

'I'm sorry,' he groaned. 'I'm so sorry.' He buried his face against her throat.

Her disappointment at not reaching that pinnacle with him faded in the knowledge that

she had at least given him pleasure, and she
caressed the dampness of his back with soothing
movements. Whether Hawk accepted the fact or
not, she belonged to him now, and she was
happy.

His eyes were dark with pain as he raised his
head to look down at her. 'There were no other
lovers for you, Whitney.' It was a statement, not
a question, her virginity seconds ago never in
doubt.

'No,' she smiled.

'I hurt you,' he rasped self-disgustedly.

'Just a little.' She didn't lie, knew he had felt
her pain.

'And after hurting you I didn't even have the
control to give you the pleasure you gave me.' He
rolled on his back at her side, one arm flung
across his eyes. 'That hasn't happened to me
since I was a teenager and I realised lovemaking
wasn't the selfish thing I'd imagined it to be! I
made better love when I was seventeen years old
than I did to you just now!'

Whitney knew there had been plenty of women
in Hawk's life before his marriage to Geraldine,
guessed that the married couple had been happy
enough physically at the start of their marriage at
least, and she didn't resent any of the women he
had known, because minutes ago Hawk had
shown her by his very lack of control that there
hadn't been any other women for a very long
time, that he certainly hadn't made love to
Geraldine the previous night.

The dark hair on his chest was curling

damply against his bronzed skin, his jaw rigid with tension beneath his upraised arm. She moved to caress the hardness of his jaw with her lips even as her fingers entangled in the thick dark hair, feeling the hardness of his nipples beneath her touch, his chest ceasing all movement before his breath was released in a ragged sigh.

'Whitney——'

'Give to me, Hawk,' she encouraged throatily. 'Give to me now!'

His arm lowered as he looked at her with darkened eyes. 'I'm not sure that I can,' he moaned. 'Contrary to what they would have us believe men aren't sexual athletes; I need time to recuperate.'

She may have been a virgin but she wasn't naïve; she knew that she could make Hawk want her again with caressing patience. And they had all night.

Her hair lay like a dark curtain against his body as she slowly began to kiss him, feeling his body tense before he relaxed with a sigh of pleasure, that tension once again evident as she moved with light kisses towards his thighs.

'Whitney!'

'Let me.' Her eyes were dark pools of need. She wanted nothing else but to give this man pleasure, to bind him to her with the only ties he would allow.

His head fell back against the pillows in defeat, helpless beneath her caresses, each one bolder than the last, until he pulled her back above him, taking one taut nipple into his mouth as it curved so temptingly towards him.

Now he was once again the master, his caresses like nothing she had ever imagined, tense with need as he kissed her, fast approaching that fiery release that had eluded her before. This time she felt an increase of that desire as his thighs took the place of his lips, no longer fearful of her ability to take him inside her, feeling as if he were the perfect half to herself.

And then she wasn't thinking at all, fire claiming her in a nerve-ending burst that set aflame her whole body, crying out her pleasure to Hawk, feeling his warmth as he joined her in the ecstasy.

This time Hawk was the one to comfort her, although his hands were unsteady as he held her against his side, spasms of passion still wracking his body, his breathing ragged.

'What have I done?' he suddenly groaned.

'What have *we* done?' she corrected huskily, her body awash with lethargy.

'I didn't just step down off that pedestal, I smashed it to pieces!' he rasped disgustedly.

She wasn't going to give him the time to regret what had happened between them, knew that if she did he would leave her. And she would have this one night with him if nothing else. She had loved him too much and for too long to give up this time with him.

'Come and wash my back for me,' she encouraged throatily, getting out of bed to hold our her hand for him to join her.

His eyes darkened as he saw the physical evidence of his lovemaking, the paleness of her skin showing signs in places of being grazed by the stubble on his jaw, her nipples a rosy red from his heated ministration, her eyes heavy with passion. It was the last that was his undoing, as he slowly followed her to the bathroom.

Their shower together led to yet more lovemaking, as Whitney had hoped that it would, and afterwards they fell into an exhausted sleep, still wrapped in each other's arms.

It was the feeling that something was different that woke her, the sunlight showing against the curtained window showing her it was morning. Hawk was still curved into the back of her body, hadn't left her while she slept as she had dreaded he would. His hand rested possessively on her breast, the gentle throb of his lower body telling her that he would soon wake to initiate another bout of the fiery lovemaking they had made their own.

And then she realised what had woken her, what was different. The yacht's engines were going; they were moving!

Hawk came awake instantly as she turned to him, a shutter coming down over his emotions after his initial flare of pleasure at seeing her in his arms. 'What is it?' He frowned.

'We're moving.' She looked puzzled. 'I thought you said——'

'A change in plans.' He turned away from her to swing his legs out of bed, his broad back to her as he spoke again. 'That was what I came to talk to you about last night.' He ran a hand through the tousled lightness of his hair. 'I seem to have been side-tracked.' He sighed heavily.

'But where are we going?' she frowned.

'Europe.'

'Europe?' she echoed dazedly. 'Where in Europe?'

He stood up to begin pulling on his clothes. 'I thought that as we have guests——'

'Guests?' she echoed again, feeling a little like an annoying child, and it was the last thing she wanted to be to Hawk now. But 'guests' could only mean one thing. 'You mean Tom Beresford and Geraldine are still on board?' Her eyes were wide with disbelief.

Hawk didn't quite meet her gaze as he at last turned to face her. 'Yes!' he bit out.

'But why?'

He looked at her coldly. 'They're my guests,' he maintained firmly.

'And I'm expected to behave myself around them,' she realised dully.

'Yes,' he rasped. 'Now I have to get back to my own suite before any of them starts wandering about.'

'Why?' she said bitterly, falling back against the pillows, staring up at the ceiling. 'They all think we're lovers anyway.'

'They may think it,' Hawk snapped. 'But that doesn't mean we have to confirm it!'

'I would have thought it would only have convinced them of our relationship if they knew you spent the night with me,' she said dully.

'Whitney,' he reasoned impatiently. 'Last night wasn't planned——'

'I know that,' she sighed heavily. 'But why have they stayed on board? Geraldine gets seasick at the sight of water!'

'She may do, but she's still on board.' Hawk looked grim.

'You still haven't told me why,' she persisted.

He shook his head regretfully. 'I can't tell you that.'

'No,' she accepted with a heavy sigh. 'I don't suppose you can.'

CHAPTER SEVEN

WHAT followed had to be the strangest day she had ever known. Geraldine was once again plagued with seasickness and was confined to her cabin, only highlighting the fact that there was something strange about the Beresfords being on board.

Because of the other woman's absence, Whitney was left alone in the company of the four men. If they could be called company! Hawk was in an uncommunicative, brooding mood, watching her when he didn't think she was aware of it. Tom Beresford was his usual arrogantly charming self, and although Alex Cordell and Glyn Briant looked as if they might have been better company the two men kept themselves pretty much in the background of things.

They were a strange collection of people, and by mid-afternoon Whitney was totally confused as to how she should act with each individual, wondering if it were only Glyn Briant and Hawk in on this plan to arrest Tom Beresford, or if Alex Cordell were in on it, too. When she said she intended to go and sunbathe on deck he was the only one to suggest joining her, and then she was sure it was only out of politeness because no one else offered.

He was a man of medium height, medium

build, with short brown hair, and dark brown eyes; in fact there was nothing in the least daunting about him. Whitney couldn't help wondering how he had come to be involved in Tom Beresford's organisation, let alone become what amounted to no more than a bodyguard!

'I'm a judo expert,' he drawled as he sensed her scrutiny.

Whitney felt her cheeks flush with colour, glad she was wearing sunglasses to shield the embarrassed dismay in her eyes. 'I'm sorry,' she grimaced. 'It's just that you seem an intelligent man ... I'm sorry.' She pulled a face. 'That sounded very rude!'

He laughed, looking younger than the late thirties or early forties he must be, a distinct gleam of amusement in his eyes now. 'I'm not in the least offended,' he told her easily. 'Some of us make our living with our brawn, some of us with our brains.' He shrugged. 'We all do what we do the best.'

She nodded. 'My father raced motor cycles; I wouldn't exactly call that cerebral!'

'So did Mr Hawkworth,' he acknowledged. 'But he's proved he can use his brawn and his brain.'

Her expression softened as she thought of the man she loved. 'Yes. I don't suppose——'

'Mind if I join you?'

She frowned up at Glyn Briant for his intrusion, having felt she could relax with Alex Cordell in a way she hadn't been able to with anyone else all day.

'Have my lounger,' Alex instantly offered, standing up. 'It's time one of us checked on Mrs Beresford's welfare anyway.'

Whitney watched him go with some regret. Hawk and Glyn had told her enough of what was happening to put her mind at rest about Hawk's involvement with Tom Beresford, but they hadn't told her enough to stop her feeling like a fish floundering out of water, and she had a feeling they weren't going to either!

'Enjoying the cruise?' Glyn drawled, making himself comfortable beside her.

'Not particularly,' she snapped, not even looking at him. 'Did you leave Hawk trying to malign himself even more for your sake?' she scorned.

'Hawk told me he would be able to handle you,' he muttered.

Her mouth twisted mockingly. 'Life is full of these little disappointments!'

'Whitney,' he sighed, his barely contained impatience forcing her to look at him. 'Behave yourself, or Hawk could be the one that gets hurt.'

Her eyes widened. 'Are you threatening me?' she gasped wonderingly.

'No,' he denied wearily. 'I doubt that would do any good in your case. But I wish to God you had stayed out of this as you were supposed to!'

'Now that I know Hawk's involved it wouldn't be possible,' she shook her head.

'If you really love him,' Glyn rasped, 'then don't fight him, help him.'

'I would,' she groaned forcefully. 'If I just knew what was going on!'

Glyn gave a frustrated sigh. 'Can't you just trust him?' he prompted.

'I do trust him,' she stated flatly.

'But not me,' he guessed, his mouth twisting. 'I realise I'd never win any medals for diplomacy,' he derided, 'but I'm good at my job——'

'Just what is your job?' she demanded frowningly.

'I can't tell you,' he sighed.

Whitney shrugged. 'Then how do you expect me to help Hawk when I don't even know what's happening half the time? You and Hawk have been involved in this together for months; I don't even know who the "good guys" are and who the "bad guys" are!'

Glyn gave a derisive smile. 'It isn't always as black and white as that any more.'

She pulled a face. 'In other words, you don't really know either!'

He laughed softly. 'You know, Hawk completely underestimated you.'

She frowned warily. 'In what way?'

Glyn shrugged. 'I think he imagined you're still a little girl he has to protect.'

Not any more he didn't. Hawk could be in no doubt of her maturity after the night they had spent together. But he had been avoiding her most of the day, and she knew he regretted losing his temper with her in such a way that he ended up by making love to her. But no matter how he tried he couldn't deny what had happened between them, and she didn't intend letting him forget it.

Glyn was watching her with narrowed eyes when she glanced back at him. 'But perhaps that isn't true any more, hm?' he prompted curiously.

She raised black brows. 'Just why did Hawk ever agree to help you in this?' She attacked, rather than defended, knowing her expression must have given her away.

Glyn's face was suddenly like a closed book, no emotion showing. 'You'll have to ask Hawk that.'

'A lot of good that would do me!' she snapped. 'He's about as confiding as a clam!'

'Did it ever occur to you that he's only trying to protect you?'

'Did it occur to either of you that I don't want to be protected!'

His eyes were bleak. 'This isn't some damned children's game——'

'As you guessed seconds ago, I'm no longer a child,' she bit out.

'That's between you and Hawk,' he rasped, standing up to leave.

'Just don't let it interfere with your work, right?' she scorned.

He leant down until his face was only inches away from hers. 'Don't attempt to sharpen your claws on me, Whitney; I've been known to savage the best of them in my time!' he warned.

She met his gaze unflinchingly. 'If anything happens to Hawk you'll find out just how sharp my claws actually are,' she returned challengingly.

A ghost of a smile lightened his eyes, easing the

tension a little. 'Hawk has definitely under-estimated you,' he murmured.

'Why don't you try telling him that?' she taunted. 'Maybe then the two of you will stop treating me like some sort of imbecile!'

Glyn whistled softly through his teeth. 'I'm glad we're on the same side . . .'

She smiled in spite of herself, sighing as her tension eased. 'Shouldn't you be getting back to the others now?' she suggested without rancour. 'You've probably been missed.'

He shrugged. 'I'm allowed to be as susceptible to a beautiful face as the next man.'

'I'm glad one of you is.' She settled her sunglasses more comfortably on the bridge of her nose, her face raised to the sun. 'Hawk seems to be having no trouble resisting.'

'Resisting what?'

Her hands tightened on the arms of her lounger, but otherwise she gave no sign that Hawk's unexpected appearance had disturbed her. 'A beautiful woman,' she drawled. 'Or have you already checked how Geraldine is today? Silly me, of course you have,' she dismissed tartly. 'It seems to be the male pastime of the day!'

Hawk looked at them questioningly. 'Who else—Alex?' He frowned.

'He went down to check on her half an hour ago,' she answered him abruptly. 'Don't tell me he hasn't come back yet?' she derided waspishly. 'Dear me, her husband isn't going to like that, is he?' she taunted. 'But the question is, which husband?' she added hardly.

'Whitney——'

'I think it's very inconsiderate of you, Hawk,' she continued, as if he hadn't interrupted her in that steely voice. 'You could at least have brought an equal amount of women and men on board. Poor Geraldine and I are having trouble coping with you all.'

'Tom wants you,' he rasped to the other man, his jaw rigid with anger.

Glyn gave a terse nod of his head. 'I enjoyed our chat, Whitney,' he mocked. 'And I'll keep a look out for the claws.'

Hawk turned back to her once the other man had gone. 'What was that about?'

Whitney gazed her fill of him from behind the protective shield of her sunglasses, loving the way the short sleeves on his shirt showed the muscular length of his bronzed arms, his dark trousers snug to his lean waist and thighs.

He looked tired, lines beside the dark shadows under his eyes, and Whitney couldn't help smiling as she recalled every moment they had spent awake together in her bed last night.

His eyes narrowed with suspicion at her humour. 'What's so funny?'

Her smile deepened at his wary aggression. 'Not funny,' she denied huskily. 'Beautiful.'

Colour darkened the leanness of his cheeks. 'Whitney, last night——'

'Was wonderful; I know.' She stood up to drape her arms about his neck, curving her body into the hardness of his. 'The best yet,' she added throatily as she raised her mouth to his.

'Best yet?' he repeated dazedly, holding her away from him. 'But——'

'It was lovely while we were here alone,' she nodded, her gaze warning. 'But there's something deliciously erotic about knowing there are other people aboard while we make love,' she murmured seductively. 'In fact, why don't we go down to my suite right now? I'm sure no one will miss us.'

A nerve pulsed in his cheeks at the deliberate way she was rubbing against his thighs. 'Whitney——'

'Sorry to interrupt.' The embarrassed voice of Alex Cordell cut in on them. 'Mr Beresford would like to talk to you,' he awkwardly told the narrow-eyed Hawk.

Hawk nodded dismissively. 'Tell him I'll be there in a moment.' His eyes glowed golden as he gazed down at Whitney once they were alone again. 'Thanks.' He sighed ruefully. 'Since you came on board I seem to have lost my taste for subterfuge.'

She ran her fingertips lightly down the rigidity of his jaw. 'How much longer does this have to go on?' she asked in a pained voice.

He sighed. 'It will all be over soon. I hope,' he added fervently.

Sadness darkened her eyes. 'Because of last night,' she guessed.

He looked away. 'I never meant for last night to happen——' He was silenced by Whitney's fingertips lightly placed against his lips. He firmly took her hand in his. 'I need to talk to you,' he told her gruffly. 'I'll come to your suite later tonight.'

Whitney smiled to herself as she fell asleep in the afternoon sunshine. Hawk may think he could come to her tonight, logically discuss and dismiss the change in their relationship, and then leave, but she knew better. Once he was alone with her in her suite he wouldn't be able to leave. Her body was filled with a warm ache at the thought of another night in his arms.

It was her new relationship with Hawk that gave her the confidence to call in and see Geraldine on her way to change for dinner. The other woman looked awful, a greenish tinge to her cheek, looking every one of her thirty-three years.

'Come to gloat?' she snapped, struggling against the pillows to sit up, the peach colour of her nightgown doing nothing for her sallow complexion.

Whitney's mouth quirked. 'Don't judge everyone else by your own actions.'

The green eyes narrowed venomously. 'Why did you come here?'

Whitney shrugged. 'As your hostess,' she deliberately baited, 'I thought it my duty to come and see how you are.'

'As you can see, I'm lousy!' Geraldine choked self-pityingly. 'I never could understand why Hawk actually enjoyed going away for days at a time in this floating hell!'

Whitney frowned, sitting down on the chair near the bed; she was wearing a loose robe over her bikini. 'We both know you've always suffered from seasickness, so why did you subject yourself to this trip?'

'I have my reasons,' Geraldine snapped. 'And in the meantime enjoy your relationship with Hawk. Such as it is,' she sneered. 'Because the moment I decide to break you two up I'll do it, just like that!' She snapped her fingers together in satisfaction.

The other woman had always had the ability to hit out at a person's weakest spot, and Whitney's uncertainty of her relationship with Hawk had been encouraged just enough to unsettle her.

She stood up. 'Your vitriolic tongue hasn't changed a bit,' she said disgustedly.

'Neither has your oh-so-transparent love for Hawk,' Geraldine jeered. 'As I said, enjoy it while you can—while I let you.'

Whitney was shaking with reaction by the time she reached her own suite. It wasn't that she wasn't a fighter—no one who really knew her could ever accuse her of that!—but her own relationship with Hawk was so tenuous, and Geraldine's hold over him had always been so destructive. As arrogant and self-assured as Hawk was she wasn't sure that this time it was going to be any different.

Dinner seemed to drag on endlessly, even Sean's attempts to tease her receiving only a ghost of her usual returned humour. She wanted to talk to Hawk, desperately, and trying to be polite to one man she despised, another she was indifferent to, despite his friendliness this afternoon, and another man who alarmed her because he and Hawk seemed to be working in the dark, was hell when all she wanted was to be alone with Hawk.

'This trip seems to be having an adverse effect on the ladies,' Tom Beresford drawled when Whitney made her excuses because of a headache. 'Thank God we reach Amsterdam tomorrow.'

Amsterdam? Whitney gave him a sharp look. They were going to Amsterdam? But why? What on earth had Hawk got himself involved in!

'Ssh,' he warned just over an hour later when he knocked on the door to her suite.

'But——'

'Let's get inside,' Glyn Briant advised impatiently. 'We're very conspicuous out here!'

Whitney frowned as the other man followed Hawk into her suite and firmly closed the door behind him. She had wanted to be alone with Hawk, not listen to him and Glyn Briant discussing Tom Beresford again. The regret in his golden eyes told her Hawk knew of her feelings and that he sympathised with them. But that didn't stop him sitting in her lounge spreading the file and photographs *she* had got together all over *her* coffee-table to go through it all very closely with Glyn Briant!

'Don't mind me,' she snapped after several minutes of their intense conversation over each photograph.

Glyn looked up at her with amused eyes. 'How about getting us some coffee; it's going to be a long night!' He looked pointedly at the tray of coffee she had had brought to her suite for Hawk and herself.

Her eyes flashed. 'There are only two cups,' she dismissed.

'That's all right,' he grinned. 'There are only two of us!'

She drew in an angry breath, wrapping her robe more firmly about her. 'Pour your own coffee, I'm going to bed!' She slammed into the adjoining room, refusing to turn around as she heard the door softly open before closing again, knowing by that elusive lime smell that Hawk had followed her.

His hands came down to rest gently against her shoulders. 'You shouldn't let him get to you,' he chided. 'Teasing you is fast becoming his favourite pastime,' he told her ruefully.

Her eyes were awash with tears as she turned to face him. 'I thought we would be alone tonight,' she said, voicing her disappointment.

'So did I.' He sighed. 'But Glyn hasn't been able to find anything detrimental in your file or photographs on the Beresfords either; he thought that a combined effort might help us solve the mystery of why it became so important you were actually threatened for it.'

'In *my* suite!'

He shrugged. 'We thought it might be less obvious. Why don't you come and help us?'

'The rule being, "if you can't beat them join them"!' she said caustically.

Hawk grimaced at her frustrated anger. 'Something like that,' he nodded.

She shook her head. 'I wouldn't even know what I was looking for.'

Hawk gently touched her cheek. 'Then just come and sit with me,' he encouraged softly.

Her anger melted as if it had never been as she drowned in the warmth of his eyes. And Glyn Briant couldn't stay in her suite *all* night—he had better not try anyway! 'Just let me put some clothes on first,' she complied huskily.

His eyes darkened as he looked at the bareness of her flesh above the V-neckline of her robe. 'What do you have on under that?' His voice was gruff.

She smiled as a nerve pulsed in his cheek. 'Absolutely nothing,' she murmured.

'God!' His hands shook slightly as he held her. 'For me?'

'I told you, Hawk, it's always been just for you.' She became lost in the golden depths of his eyes. 'Are you sure you can't go through those things with Glyn another time?' she encouraged breathlessly.

He drew in a ragged breath, shaking his head regretfully. 'We reach Amsterdam tomorrow—'

'But *what's* going to happen in Amsterdam?' she groaned in her confusion.

'We aren't sure yet,' he grimaced. 'We can only keep hoping.'

'But——'

'Let me just take one look at you.' He released the belt at her waist to push aside her robe, his breath catching in his throat at the golden beauty of her slender nakedness. One hand moved instinctively to cup her breast, knowing the full weight of her. 'One look isn't going to be enough!' he groaned, bending his head to claim the nipple held up to him.

The warmth Whitney had longed for all day enveloped her, and she clung to him weakly, supported only by his arm on her back.

The soft rap on the door broke them apart, Glyn barely giving Whitney time to refasten her robe before opening the door. 'I don't mean to be a bore, Hawk,' he sighed, 'but we do only have until tomorrow to sort this mess out.'

Hawk stood slightly in front of Whitney, partly shielding her from the other man's gaze. 'I'll be there in a minute, Glyn,' he bit out.

'That's good of you,' the other man rasped icily.

Hawk crossed the room in angry strides. 'Don't ever,' he ground out, '*ever* walk in on Whitney and I like that again,' he warned harshly, his eyes hard as gold nuggets.

Glyn shrugged. 'I'm sorry.'

Hawk nodded abruptly. 'I'm sure Whitney appreciates your apology,' he said softly. 'Now I *will* be rejoining you in a few minutes.' He watched the other man with narrowed eyes as he closed the door behind him. 'I'm sorry, Whitney.' He turned to her once they were alone, regret in his eyes. 'Once I was alone with you I just couldn't seem to stop myself.' He touched her flushed cheeks.

She nodded. 'I'll dress and join you soon.'

'Whitney——'

'It's all right, Hawk.' She smiled tremulously. 'There will be time for us later—won't there?'

'I hope so.' He nodded wearily. 'Don't be too long,' he added gruffly.

They must have drunk pints, rather than cups, of coffee during the next few hours, Whitney going to the galley to make it as Sean had gone to bed. As the two men laboured over the photographs Whitney sat and watched them, not sure what it was they were looking for, and they seemed loath to confide in her.

'I think I've found the pattern,' Glyn suddenly exclaimed. 'My God . . .!' He gathered up several of the photographs checking the dates which Whitney had meticulously written on the back of each one. 'Hawk!' He thrust the photographs at the other man.

Hawk seemed to pale as he took in the significance of what he was seeing. 'I don't believe it,' he told the other man harshly.

'Check the dates,' Glyn encouraged grimly. 'There's no mistake. It was right there under our noses all the time!' he added forcefully.

'What was?' Whitney frowned at the two men. 'What is it?'

'Nothing that need concern you.' Hawk thrust the photographs back at Glyn. 'Unless she admits it I won't believe she was involved,' he grated.

She? Geraldine? My God, if the other woman were physically involved in her husband's corruption Hawk would never allow anything to happen to her. This was obviously something he hadn't planned on happening!

Glyn packed the damning photographs away in the file with the written reports. 'It explains why we've never been able to catch him; we've been looking in the wrong places!'

'She may be selfish and a first-class bitch, but I don't believe she's capable of this,' Hawk insisted again grimly, his face still very pale.

'Photographs don't lie, Hawk,' the other man said regretfully.

Hawk drew in an angry breath. 'At least give her the benefit of the doubt, man.'

Glyn shrugged. 'It isn't me she's going to have to convince of her innocence, you know that.'

'You aren't going to arrest her——'

'You know I'll have to,' Glyn bit out. 'Look, she isn't your responsibility any more, Hawk. Let Beresford worry about her. Whitney is the woman in your life now,' he reminded forcefully.

Hawk looked at her as if he had never seen her before, let alone made love to her.

'Remember the reason you came in on this,' Glyn added pointedly.

Hawk's eyes became dull. 'I'll never forget that,' he rasped. 'It's another reason I'll never accept Geraldine's involvement.'

She had known it had to be Geraldine's guilt Hawk was protesting so strongly, and the knowledge that he could so defend the other woman left her with an emptiness inside she had never wanted to feel again, having known that same desolation a year ago when Hawk had put her out of his life. Hawk was never going to get over his love for Geraldine.

'That isn't for us to decide,' Glyn shrugged.

'But——'

'Sleep on it, Hawk,' the other man instructed harshly. 'You'll see I have no choice.'

'If I thought about it for a year it still wouldn't change my opinion,' Hawk rasped.

Glyn gave a weary sigh. 'Try and talk some sense into him, Whitney.' He shook his head. 'If anyone can do it you can.'

An uneasy silence filled the room once he had gone. Whitney didn't know what to say; what *could* she say to the man who was her lover but was so obviously still in love with his ex-wife?

He spoke suddenly. 'We'll have to postpone our chat. All this has—changed, things a little.' He ran an agitated hand through the thickness of his hair, the light overhead gleaming on the golden strands among the dark blond.

Whitney didn't feel as if they had anything left to talk about now. 'Yes,' she accepted dully. 'I'm sorry—that Geraldine is involved,' she added weakly, not knowing what else to say.

He swallowed hard. 'Would you—I'd like to——' He broke off, shaking his head.

'Yes?' she prompted sharply.

His eyes were dark with pain. 'Would you make love to me?'

If he had asked her to walk over hot coals, jump into a pool full of sharks, sit in a room with a poisonous snake, she might have found it easier to say yes to any of them than she did to the thought of making love with him after the way he had just shown his love for Geraldine. And yet she couldn't say no to him, never had been able to deny him anything he asked of her.

'Forget I said that,' he dismissed harshly as he saw the hurt bewilderment in her face. 'It would just be another mistake to add to the many I've already made with you.'

She flinched at that description being applied to the most wonderful night of her life. 'Then you make love to me,' she prompted, her violet gaze steady on his. 'I'd like to be close to you tonight.' After tomorrow she felt sure there would be no other nights together like this.

Hawk drew in a ragged breath. 'I think I should tell you——'

'Don't tell me anything,' she put in quickly. 'Let's just go to bed.'

'Maybe you're right,' he sighed heavily. 'God, how I wish you had stayed out of this.'

'And that you had never made love to me?'

'I'll never regret that,' he said with certainty. 'I fought it, but I'll never regret it.'

He didn't seem to realise how much he had hurt her with his defence of Geraldine, how much he was hurting her now with his reluctance to at least give his body to her one more time. But there would be time for pain later; now belonged to them, and tomorrow was time enough to let him return to Geraldine.

Hawk made love to her with an intensity that made her head spin, each caress, each heated word, having special meaning, as if he couldn't get enough of her, wanted to imprint every part of her in his brain, as if he, too, regretted that they would never be together like this again. Whitney knew it couldn't really be so, but she loved him nonetheless, gave back every caress, longing to tell him of her love but daring only to tell him how much he pleased her.

Tonight he didn't want to sleep at all, repeating the sensual ritual, even more slowly this time, creating even more tension, until Whitney begged him to end the torture.

They made love with fierce intensity time and time again, both of them wishing away the dawn, not wanting to relinquish the magic of the night.

But dawn stayed away for no man—or woman—and Hawk and Whitney were only mere mortals allowed a brief glimpse of heaven. They had no choice but to face the day ahead.

Hawk lingered in her suite even after he had showered and dressed, his expression remote. 'Whatever happens today, if it happens, stay out of it, all right?' he instructed harshly.

'But what's *going* to happen?' she demanded frustratedly, 'Can't you at least tell me what all this is about now?'

His eyes became chilled, 'Drugs,' he stated flatly.

She blinked her surprise, frowning. 'But I thought——'

'I know what you thought, Whitney,' he rasped. 'And it was better that you did. But things could get nasty today, and I don't want you getting in the line of fire.'

She swallowed hard, her eyes wide. 'Could there be actual shooting?'

'Who knows?' he sighed heavily. 'Anything could happen when Glyn challenges him.'

If Geraldine was somehow involved in helping her second husband in drug-smuggling, no wonder Hawk was so upset!

CHAPTER EIGHT

'WHAT happens now?' Whitney faced Hawk across the breakfast table the two of them shared, the others having eaten earlier. Neither of them had any real appetite for the food on the serving unit, Whitney stirring sugar into her coffee, Hawk looking bleak.

They had been moored in Amsterdam for some time now; there was a curious watchfulness about Hawk that made her uneasy.

'We wait,' he shrugged.

'For what?'

'Who the hell knows?' He stood up impatiently. 'Glyn is running this show.'

She looked up at him with troubled eyes. 'Do you still believe Geraldine is innocent?'

He gave a ragged sigh. 'I don't know that either. Those photographs ...' He shook his head.

'Yes?' she prompted softly.

'They were pretty damning,' he rasped. 'But I know Geraldine hates drug pushers as much as I do. She liked Dan——'

'My father?' Whitney questioned sharply. 'What does he have to do with this?'

Hawk's eyes were hooded, making their expression unreadable. 'Nothing,' he bit out forcefully.

'But you just said——'

'Hawk, he wants to go ashore now.' Glyn Briant burst into the room now, his face flushed.

Hawk stiffened. 'Geraldine?'

'She's staying on board,' Glyn dismissed. 'She feels too ill to get off.'

'At least that's something!' Hawk shrugged his regret at Whitney as she watched them. 'I have to go, Whitney; we'll talk when I get back.'

She was still too stunned by the mention of her father in connection with Tom Beresford and Geraldine to be able to formulate an answer. Her father had never been involved in drugs, so what was Hawk talking about?

'Whitney?' he prompted concernedly.

She blinked up at him dazedly. 'I don't understand——'

'Kiss her and let's go, Hawk,' Glyn instructed harshly. 'I'm not going to lose him now.'

Hawk's eyes were narrowed. 'You think he's going to make the exchange himself?'

'With Geraldine sick he'll have to.' Glyn's mouth twisted triumphantly.

Hawk looked down regretfully at Whitney, his hands on her shoulders as he drew her up in front of him for his kiss, lingering over the caress, his eyes dark with passion when he finally raised his head. 'Stay away from Geraldine while I'm gone,' he rasped.

'I will,' she agreed dazedly. 'But I wish you would tell me——'

'We're ready to leave now, Mr Hawkworth.' Glyn's voice had changed, become more formal,

and as Whitney turned curiously towards him she
realised why; Tom Beresford and Alex Cordell
had joined him.

'Fine.' Hawk nodded abruptly before com-
pelling Whitney to look at him once again. 'I'll
see you later,' he promised huskily.

Whitney watched the men leave, still puzzled
by Hawk's unexpected mention of her father.
What was the connection? If there were one. She
and her father had only spoken of drugs once that
she could ever remember, and he had despised
the illegal use of them.

She was still leaning over the rail where she
had watched the departure of the four men when
she knew she was no longer alone, that slightly
elusive perfume Geraldine always wore telling of
her presence.

'Where is everyone?' she demanded caustically.

Whitney slowly turned to face her. The other
woman looked beautiful in the lemon-coloured
sundress, her hair taking on a redder glow than
usual. But if you looked closely beneath the ex-
pertly applied make-up it was possible to see the
lines of strain and the slightly sallow tinge to her
skin that were remnants of her recent seasickness.

'Well?' Geraldine snapped as Whitney continued to look at her.

Hawk had asked her to stay away from
Geraldine while he was gone; he hadn't told her
what to do if Geraldine sought her out! She
straightened. 'Well what, Geraldine?' she drawled
derisively.

Anger flared in the deep green eyes. 'Where are

the others?' she bit out.

Whitney shrugged. 'Gone.'

'Gone?' Geraldine repeated incredulously. 'What do you mean, gone? Where have they gone?' she demanded impatiently.

'I would have thought that was obvious.' She looked pointedly ashore.

Geraldine's mouth firmed angrily. 'I don't believe you,' she scorned.

She shrugged. 'Please yourself.'

The other woman frowned at her. 'I don't know what game you're playing, but——'

'I'm past the age of playing games, Geraldine,' she rasped. 'Except those that involve Hawk; if you want him then you're going to have to fight me for him,' she warned grimly.

'And why should I possibly want a man who doesn't want me?' Geraldine returned absently, looking frowningly over the side.

'He loves you——'

Geraldine gave her a pitying look. 'Even when we were married he didn't love me,' she dismissed scornfully. 'I have no reason to think that will ever change.'

'I don't believe that,' Whitney instantly scorned.

'That's up to you,' the other woman shrugged. 'I'm quite indifferent to both you and Hawk,' she added in a bored voice. '*And* what you choose to believe or disbelieve.'

'But——'

'Are you sure the men went ashore?' Geraldine demanded in disbelief.

'I told you——'

'How long ago did they leave?' the other woman asked agitatedly.

Whitney shrugged. 'An hour or so ago. I thought you were too sick to go with them.' She frowned.

'Damn him!' Geraldine didn't seem to hear what she said, her eyes blazing with fury. 'What's he up to?' she muttered to herself. 'I was supposed to go with him. I——' She glared resentfully at Whitney as she seemed to become aware of the fact that she wasn't alone. A dozen emotions flickered across the beautiful face, predominant among them anger and uncertainty. 'Have one of the crew let me know when they get back,' she snapped before going back down to her suite.

It was obvious from the conversation that Geraldine hadn't intended remaining on board when her husband went into Amsterdam, that Tom Beresford had deliberately left her behind. Why? It was also obvious from this conversation that Geraldine was deeply embroiled in her husband's corruption.

Strange, Whitney hadn't found even a hint of a connection between Tom Beresford and drug trafficking during her investigation. True, she hadn't been looking for it, but all the same ... There had been plenty of rumours about blackmail and pay-offs, but she hadn't actually found any real proof of them, either. She hoped Hawk and Glyn knew what they were doing.

Most of all she hoped Hawk would be able to accept Geraldine's guilt.

*   *   *

'If you would concentrate a little more, darlin', you wouldn't be losing so badly,' Sean chided, once again claiming the money from the middle of the table to join his already abundant pile of coins.

Whitney gave a wan smile as she drew her attention back to the card game they were playing. 'I don't think forty pence will break me!' she drawled.

Sean had found her wandering about on deck an hour ago, and insisted on sitting down to play cards with her. It had been a favourite pastime of theirs during voyages in the past, but today Whitney could think of nothing but Hawk and the danger he might be in at this very moment. God, how she wished he had taken her with him; anything would be better than sitting here worrying about him.

Geraldine was obviously impatient for the men's return, too, coming up on deck a couple of times to pace up and down impatiently before returning to her suite with an angry toss of her head.

'Let's raise the bets to a penny a time,' Sean suggested with a twinkle in his eyes. 'Make it more interesting.'

'You know Hawk's rules,' she teased. 'Half-pennies or we go back to matchsticks!'

'But you're a big girl now,' Sean complained as he dealt the cards.

She sobered, her expression becoming shadowed. Yes, she was a big girl now, her second night with Hawk had only confirmed that;

but Hawk continued to treat her as someone he had to protect rather than someone he could share his troubles with. Much as that rankled, she knew that, if only he would love her a little in return, she would be happy to let him protect her for the rest of their lives.

She blushed as she looked up to find Sean watching her anxiously. 'OK, a penny it is,' she said brightly. 'But watch out, I feel my luck changing!'

During the next hour she lost another ninety pence, ruefully agreeing with Sean when he suggested ending the decidedly one-sided game. She was too worried about Hawk to think of anything else. The four men had been gone for hours now, lunchtime having come and gone; what on earth could they be doing all this time?

She was in her cabin when she heard the sound of the car returning, and she rushed over to the window to see that there were only two men inside. And she couldn't make out in the dark interior which two it was!

She almost collided with Geraldine as the two of them rushed out into the passageway and up to the deck, the other woman white with tension as she pushed in front of Whitney to run up the stairway first.

Whitney arrived on deck in time to see Hawk— and Tom Beresford—stepping on board!

Geraldine seemed to go grey, her gaze locked with the coldly chilling one of her husband. 'Oh, my God . . .' She breathed raggedly at the expression in his eyes.

'Yes, indeed, my dear,' Tom Beresford drawled softly. 'Not what you were expecting, is it?'

Geraldine moistened her lips, regaining a little of her usual control. 'I—er—you left earlier before I had a chance to join you.'

Her husband gave an acknowledging inclination of his head. 'By design, I assure you.'

Temper flared in the dark green eyes. 'But I wanted to come with you,' Geraldine complained.

Tom Beresford's eyes took on an icy hardness. 'I'm aware of what you wanted, Geraldine,' he rasped. 'Unfortunately it's no longer possible.'

Whitney glanced at Hawk, her initial pleasure in seeing him alive and well turning to confusion at this strange conversation between husband and wife. Hawk returned her gaze blankly.

'Tom——'

'I think it might be better if we went to our suite and discussed this in private,' Geraldine's husband interrupted her coldly.

Her eyes widened. 'No.' She shook her head, backing away from him. 'Hawk,'—she gave him a look of desperation—'don't let him do this to me!'

Hawk's mouth twisted. 'If you're lucky, Geraldine,' he drawled uninterestedly, 'he may decide to only beat you twice a week for the rest of your life!'

'Hawk!' Whitney gasped, moving quickly to his side. 'Isn't Glyn going to arrest them or—or something?' she demanded.

'No,' he mocked, his arm moving about her shoulders to hold her against him.

'Arrest me?' Geraldine became flushed with anger. 'Why should Glyn Briant want to arrest me?'

'He's an undercover policeman, my dear,' Tom Beresford drawled mockingly.

'So?' Her eyes widened indignantly.

Her husband's mouth tightened angrily. 'So he's been persuaded to wait until we get back to England before arresting you,' he bit out.

'Don't be ridiculous,' Geraldine snapped. 'I'm not guilty of anything.'

'You don't call carrying drugs "guilty of anything"?' Hawk rasped, his eyes bleak.

'Drugs?' Geraldine repeated dazedly. 'Have the two of you been drinking?'

'No—but I'm about to start!' Her husband strode past her and into the lounge, pouring himself a large glass of whisky before swallowing it down. 'You can stop the act now, Geraldine,' he told her wearily. 'The police know everything.'

Whitney couldn't understand why Glyn was waiting until they reached England before arresting this couple. Neither could she understand why he wasn't here now. She walked beside Hawk as they followed the other couple into the lounge.

Tom drained his glass of whisky and poured himself another one. 'For God's sake say something, Geraldine,' he thundered. 'Even if it's only that you're sorry!' he scorned.

Geraldine stiffened. 'How can I be sorry for something I don't even know I've done!'

Her husband gave a snort of disgust. 'I don't know why I ever allowed myself to fall in love with you,' he rasped. 'You're nothing but a selfish, deceitful bitch!'

'Hawk!' Geraldine prompted indignantly.

He shrugged, his expression remote. 'He's owed this, at the very least,' he sighed.

The green eyes flashed. 'I do not care to have my private life discussed in front of Whitney,' she snapped angrily.

'Do you not?' her husband challenged.

'No!'

'That's a pity—because she's staying!' Tom Beresford bit out forcefully. 'God, she's more of a woman than you'll ever be, for all that she's over ten years younger,' he scorned. 'She was willing to stand by Hawk, even if he was a criminal; you've never cared for anyone or anything but yourself.'

Geraldine blinked. 'You mean—you mean Hawk *was* pretending all the time?'

Tom's mouth twisted. 'Now you're starting to get the idea,' he derided.

She swallowed hard. 'But I thought——My God!' She glared her dislike of Hawk. 'I should have known you would never really be involved in——' She broke off abruptly, her mouth tight.

'Yes, my dear?' her husband prompted softly. 'Why don't you tell us what Hawk would never have been involved in but that *you* surely were?

Geraldine turned her back on them, breathing

deeply. 'I don't have to tell you anything,' she dismissed scornfully.

'No?' Her husband swung her around. 'You'll tell everything, damn you,' he bit out fiercely. 'Hawk's part in this may have all been pretence, but mine certainly wasn't!'

Geraldine visibly paled at the threat, suddenly looking old. 'You knew what I was like before you asked me to marry you——'

'I knew you were promiscuous, not that you were stupid!' her husband snarled.

'How dare you?' Her eyes flashed.

'Quite easily,' he assured her contemptuously.

'Why is it that men are always so quick to pass on the blame for their wife's infidelity?' Geraldine snapped. 'Hawk was the same. He spent all of his time working, and when he wasn't working he was with that brat every minute of the——'

'Geraldine!' Hawk thundered, his arm tightening about Whitney's shoulders.

Whitney could have told him that he had no need to feel indignant on her behalf; she had always known of Geraldine's opinion of her. Brat was quite a mild insult compared with some of the things she had called her in the past. Nevertheless, she felt warmed by Hawk's instantaneous defence of her. Even if she did find all of this conversation still very much a puzzle!

'Well, you were,' Geraldine maintained resentfully. 'And Tom was no better. Before we were married we were together all the time, but as soon as I became his wife I was just another possession he quickly lost interest in.'

'I'm sure that if you consider marriage the cause of the trouble between us a divorce could easily be arranged,' her husband told her coldly.

Geraldine gave a ragged sigh. 'I know I'm selfish and demanding, but I can't change the way I am.'

'You know damn well there's a lot more involved in this than your affair with another man,' Tom Beresford rasped.

'I never said I was having an affair,' she flushed.

Her husband gave a harsh sigh. 'Do you have any idea of the penalty for drug smuggling?' His eyes were narrowed.

'I wish you would stop saying——'

'Cordell was arrested this morning,' Tom cut in coldly.

If Geraldine looked stunned by this revelation Whitney knew she didn't look any better. Alex Cordell, Tom Beresford's second 'minder', had been arrested? She looked up at Hawk questioningly, receiving an encouraging smile from him before he turned back to the other couple.

'Alex . . .?' Geraldine repeated weakly.

'Your lover,' her husband taunted hardly. 'The man who has been sharing your bed every time I didn't; the man who joined you on your weekends in Switzerland so that the two of you could check on his bank account there; the man you've been carrying drugs for!'

CHAPTER NINE

'THAT'S a lie!' Geraldine finally managed to gasp in a strangulated cry.

'Which part of it?' her husband said disgustedly, suddenly looking old.

Geraldine couldn't quite seem to meet his gaze. 'All of it!'

Tom shook his head sadly, no longer the arrogantly confident man Whitney had met for lunch several days ago. 'I've known for months that Cordell was your lover,' he told Geraldine contemptuously.

Whitney knew there was still a lot to be explained, but the relief of knowing it was Alex Cordell who was Geraldine's lover was enough for her to give Hawk a blinding smile. Emotion flickered in his eyes before it was quickly brought under control, his attention drawn reluctantly back to the other couple.

'Then why didn't you say something?' Geraldine scorned disbelievingly.

The pale blue eyes became icily cold. 'Do you think I've enjoyed having to stand back and watch you make a fool of me?' he bit out. 'I've lost count of the amount of times I would have liked to wring your lovely neck for you! But there was so much more involved than my pride,' he rasped. 'Did you know that my first wife died because of a drug overdose?' he challenged.

Geraldine frowned. 'I knew she died suddenly, but not how. But why do you keep going on about drugs?' she dismissed. 'I've always despised people who deal in drugs. Tell him, Hawk.'

He shrugged. 'I told myself for some time, but the evidence doesn't lie.'

'What evidence?' Geraldine snapped.

'Parcels that you've carried to various countries for Cordell,' Hawk rasped. 'Whitney unwittingly photographed him handing the parcels over to you several times,' he added grimly.

Green eyes narrowed venomously on Whitney. 'You had no right to spy on me,' Geraldine bit out.

'Is that why you had Cordell threaten her?' Hawk challenged.

Geraldine's mouth tightened. 'All I wanted was the photographs of Alex and I together; I couldn't let Tom see them without his realising that I——'

'Yes?' her husband prompted softly.

'That I was having an affair with Alex, damn it!' she acknowledged resentfully.

Tom's mouth twisted. 'Progress indeed,' he derided bitterly.

'But that's all it was,' she flared. 'This business about drug smuggling is nonsense.'

'I never took you for a fool, Geraldine,' her husband said wearily.

'I'm not!' she glared at him. 'Alex made time

for me when you couldn't—or wouldn't. He was kind. He——'

'He was using you,' Tom said disgustedly. 'He didn't want those photographs back from Whitney because they incriminated him in an affair with you; he knew they could damn him in a much more serious crime.' His eyes narrowed. 'Since you refuse to think those parcels contained drugs, just what did you think you were carrying?'

Once again Geraldine's gaze avoided meeting his. 'I don't have to tell you that.'

'You either tell me or I'll let the police have you right now,' he grated.

Geraldine paled again. 'Antiques!' she spat out.

'Antiques?' both Tom and Hawk echoed incredulously.

Geraldine's head went back challengingly. 'Not just any antiques; specialised items requested by certain clients——'

Her husband's humourless laugh interrupted her. 'You can't really believe that!'

Geraldine flushed at his unmistakable derision. 'Just because Alex worked as a bodyguard for a living is no reason to suppose he was stupid,' she flashed. 'He has a fantastic collection of antique silver himself——'

'Bought with other peoples' lives,' her husband rasped. 'He dealt in death and destruction—and for the last few months you've been helping him!'

'No, I——Tom?' Concern replaced Geraldine's anger as her husband seemed to crumple and fall, going down on her knees beside him as he lay on the floor.

Whitney reached the other man's side at the same time as Hawk did, alarmed by the grey tinge to his cheeks, pain making his eyes a dark cloudy blue.

'Tablets,' he managed to choke.

Geraldine searched frantically through his coat pockets while Hawk loosened his tie and unbuttoned his shirt. 'Dear God, what have I done?' Geraldine groaned as she anxiously watched her husband take one of the tablets she had found, his colour returning slightly to normal after only a few minutes.

'We should get him to bed,' Whitney told them calmly. 'Call a doctor——'

'No doctor,' Tom managed a wan smile. 'Although the bed sounds a good idea.'

The coolly confident Geraldine seemed to have fallen to pieces, Stephen Hollister helping Hawk to carry her husband down to his suite.

'I really think you should see a doctor, Tom.' Hawk frowned down at the other man as he lay on top of the bedclothes.

'I'll be fine,' Tom assured him, looking better by the minute. 'I've had these attacks before——'

'When?' Geraldine demanded to know. 'You never told me about them!'

His mouth twisted. 'I didn't want to worry you.'

'You didn't think I had a right to know my husband was ill?' she frowned.

He gave a rueful smile. 'At the beginning I

didn't want to make it obvious you were marrying a man old enough to be your father; lately—well, I think your affair with Cordell speaks for itself!'

'Oh, Tom!' Geraldine groaned, swallowing hard.

'Tears?' He frowned his confusion at the watery sheen to her eyes.

'Of course,' she choked. 'I love you!'

His mouth thinned. 'You have a damned funny way of showing it!'

'I——'

'Whitney and I will wait in the lounge for you, Geraldine,' Hawk cut in briskly. 'You're sure about the doctor?' he asked, frowning his concern for the other man.

'Sure.' Tom smiled at him reassuringly, glancing ruefully at Whitney. 'If I'm not mistaken you have some explaining of your own to do,' he derided.

'Oh, he definitely has,' Whitney nodded determinedly. 'He let me go on thinking you were an English version of Al Capone!'

Tom Beresford chuckled weakly. 'I quite enjoyed playing the role.'

'Hawk isn't going to think it's funny in a few minutes,' she promised.

Tom laughed softly. 'I *do* admire your taste in women, Hawk!'

Hawk smiled ruefully. 'Whitney is her own woman—and I think she's about to give me hell!'

She did feel a little like kicking his other shin; she also felt like screaming for his lack of confidence in her. Although now that she realised Tom Beresford's real role perhaps it was as well that Hawk hadn't confided in her; she always had been lousy at hiding her true feelings, and it wouldn't have done if she had actually seemed to like Tom.

Not that she intended letting Hawk get away with his deceit of her that easily; he could have been a little more honest with her than he had been. She returned his gaze with steady condemnation once they were back in the lounge.

He sighed. 'I'll start at the beginning——'

'That might be nice!'

He grimaced at her heavily laced sarcasm. 'I told you what I could, Whitney.'

'Which wasn't a whole lot!' She had felt like a spectator at an Agatha Christie film since he and Tom Beresford had arrived back alone, the guilty person far from the one she had been led to believe! Hawk wasn't going to get away with treating her like a child, not this time.

'No,' he acknowledged heavily. 'But Cordell is a very dangerous man, and I didn't want you at risk.' He shook his head. 'Geraldine has no idea how dispensable she was becoming to him. I think she really does believe she was only carrying antiques!'

Whitney was sure, much as she disliked the other woman, that her disbelief about the drugs had been genuine.

'She even gave Cordell your home telephone number believing he just wanted to retrieve the photographs that linked the two of them in an affair,' Hawk grated. 'As soon as Martin told me about that call I knew I had to keep you with me until all this was over. I got my face slapped and my shin kicked for my trouble!'

'How was I to know I'd actually photographed Alex Cordell passing on drugs?' Whitney shuddered at the realisation of the danger she had been in. It still seemed incredible to her that Alex Cordell was responsible; he had seemed such a nice man the few times they had spoken together.

'It took quite a while for Glyn and I to realise what it was he wanted from you,' Hawk grimaced.

'It all seems so—complicated.' Whitney frowned.

'It was all very simple to start with,' he sighed. 'Then Geraldine met Tom and fell in love with him, and you refused to give up your story on Tom.'

'I still don't understand how you became involved with Glyn in the first place.' She shook her head.

'Anyone selling drugs should be prevented from doing it.' Hawk's expression was bleak.

'I agree, but why did you become involved?' She frowned.

'Why not?' he returned distantly.

'Hawk!'

He sighed. 'A friend of mine died because someone supplied him with drugs.'

'A friend of yours . . .?' she repeated faintly.

'Yes,' he confirmed almost aggressively.

There was a pounding inside her head, her

breathing shallow and erratic. 'My father?' she choked.

'I do have other friends beside your father,' Hawk rasped.

'Yes, I know. But——'

'It wasn't your father, Whitney,' he cut in firmly. 'It was just a friend.'

Whitney wasn't convinced he was telling her the truth, but other than calling him a liar—which wouldn't encourage him to tell her anything—she had no way of making him confide more to her about this 'friend' of his. Besides, she refused to believe her father could have been involved in this in any way.

'What happened?' she prompted frowningly.

'It wasn't easy, but I found out from other people he was supplying that Alex Cordell was providing the drugs,' he explained grimly. 'But he's an elusive man; he has used his cover as Tom's bodyguard for years to get him to the places he wanted to go, and I couldn't even get close to him. That was when Glyn approached me. He and Tom had been working together to try and get evidence on him that would put him away for life, to no avail.'

'Alex Cordell supplied Tom's wife, too?' she realised sadly.

'Yes.'

'And I still thought it was Tom you were after,' she said self-disgustedly.

'It was better that way,' Hawk nodded.

'Not for me,' she sighed ruefully. 'I've been despising the wrong man!'

'It's because Cordell is so unobtrusive that he's proved so elusive,' Hawk explained grimly. 'Poor Tom has been cultivating his "Al Capone" image for years, just waiting for the time Cordell decided to take on a partner in what was becoming a very risky business for him. But when that failed to draw Cordell out——'

'They decided to use you,' she realised drily.

'I've been working on him for almost two years,' he admitted with a sigh, 'trying to convince him that my frequent trips on *Freedom* would be a perfect cover for the transfer of drugs. A few weeks ago I finally got him to agree to a trial run.'

'And I came along and almost ruined it,' Whitney said ruefully.

'Things looked a bit shaky for a while,' he conceded. 'But in the end it was producing the photographs he wanted that convinced him I was on the level.'

'I still can't believe it was him all the time.' She shook her head dazedly.

'His very innocuousness has been his best cover. It took Tom years to realise that his own employee was responsible for his wife's death, that Cordell was using his travels abroad with him to transport the drugs.' Hawk looked bleak. 'Tom wanted to kill him, but Glyn convinced him he could achieve more by working alongside him, that it wasn't just Cordell they had to catch but his contacts, too. It hasn't been easy for Tom to restrain himself at times, especially when Geraldine became involved with Cordell. It wasn't until Glyn and I saw those photographs last night that we realised Cordell was using Geraldine to carry the drugs.'

Whitney looked at him searchingly; if Tom Beresford had found it difficult when Geraldine had an affair with Alex Cordell, how had Hawk felt?

'Hawk, why——?'

He was looking past her now, towards the door. 'Tom?' he rasped.

'He would like to talk to you,' Geraldine told him gruffly. 'If you and Whitney have finished, of course,' she added, with a return of her usual bitchiness.

Hawk's mouth tightened. 'I hope you realise that it's only because of respect for Tom's feelings that Glyn hasn't had you arrested already?'

Green eyes flashed. 'I told Alex that he shouldn't trust you, that I didn't believe all that rubbish about excitement and adventure you had been handing him! I *knew* you were the type that's kind to animals and children, that helps little old ladies cross the road!'

Hawk looked at her with narrowed eyes. 'Unluckily for him he chose not to believe you.'

Some of the fight went out of Geraldine. 'I really didn't know he was into drugs,' she told Hawk pleadingly. 'He did tell me it was antiques I was carrying; you have to believe that, Hawk.'

'No, I don't,' he dismissed coldly. 'It's the court you have to convince. Tom may want to believe it because he loves you, but *I* don't have to do anything!'

'Hawk, listen to me——'

'I don't think I can right now,' he rasped disgustedly. 'Maybe by the time we reach England I might be able to, but not now!' He strode from the room.

Whitney wished she could leave the lounge, too, but seated as she was she couldn't make a move without being too obvious about it. As it was, her fidgeting brought Geraldine's attention to her.

'Well?' the other woman challenged resentfully.

She moistened her lips. 'Well what?' she prevaricated.

Geraldine's mouth twisted mockingly. 'Aren't you going to tell me what a bitch I am?'

Whitney bristled at the other woman's scorn. 'I never believe in stating the obvious,' she returned coldly.

To her surprise Geraldine gave a shaky laugh. 'God, how you've changed from that timid little creature so eager to please whom Hawk brought to our home seven years ago,' she said almost admiringly.

'I was looking for a mother figure,' she defended.

'And instead you found a selfish witch,' Geraldine drawled. 'I was only twenty-six, I didn't want to be a surrogate mother to a fifteen-year-old!'

'You made that perfectly obvious!' Whitney recalled bitterly.

Green eyes shot flames of anger. 'I also didn't want to share my husband with an infatuated child!'

Colour darkened her cheeks. 'It wasn't infatuation with Hawk,' she refuted. 'It was just that after my father died he seemed to be all I had to cling on to.'

'You don't have to pretend with me, Whitney,' Geraldine derided hardly. 'I know the signs of loving Hawk only too well.'

'You?' she scorned, sure this woman didn't know the meaning of the emotion.

Geraldine stiffened. 'I loved him once!'

'I find that very hard to believe,' Whitney dismissed scathingly.

'Then why do you suppose I stayed married to him?' Geraldine demanded.

'Money. The power of being Mrs James Hawkworth,' Whitney scorned.

'At the end, maybe,' the other woman conceded heavily. 'But only because Hawk had shown me that he could never love me as I loved him.'

'Never love——! You don't know what you're talking about,' Whitney dismissed heavily.

Geraldine's mouth twisted. 'I don't think I'm the one guilty of that. Of a lot of other things, maybe, but where Hawk is concerned I've always known what I was talking about. He never loved me; we only got married because I was pregnant——'

'*What?*' Whitney gasped.

'Pregnant,' Geraldine repeated derisively. 'I

was something of a motor-cycle groupie in those days, following the drivers from race to race, sleeping with any of them that I could.'

'My father . . .?'

Geraldine shrugged. 'Why not? I liked him very much, as it happens. If he hadn't known me for exactly what I was I might have become your stepmama after all,' she derided. 'But it was Hawk I wanted. He was the most exciting, most elusive, of all of them; held himself above taking advantage of what so many women offered him. He became a challenge to me. And it didn't hurt that he was heir to the Hawkworth millions either,' she derided. 'But he wasn't interested.'

'Then how——'

'I caught him in a weak moment,' Geraldine told her triumphantly. 'One of his friends was seriously injured in an accident on the circuit, and I made sure I was conveniently around when he needed company to help him forget when his friend died. A pregnancy was something neither of us counted on. But being Hawk he did the honourable thing and married me!'

Whitney was very pale. 'But I——There was no baby.' She frowned her puzzlement.

'I miscarried,' Geraldine shrugged. 'At four months. Once again Hawk was the gentleman.' Her mouth twisted. 'He didn't divorce me when the reason for our marriage no longer existed. But in every way that mattered our marriage was over.'

For years Whitney had thought Hawk was so

deeply in love with Geraldine that he didn't want another woman in his life, and now she found he had *never* loved his wife.

She didn't understand him, doubted she ever would.

CHAPTER TEN

THE week after their return to England fell into a pattern. And Whitney had never been so bored, doing nothing, in her life.

They had left Amsterdam that same afternoon, had cruised down the North Sea Canal to Ijmuiden before passing out to open sea and back to England. It had been a faster cruise back, only one night spent on board, a night when Whitney spent the night in her bedroom and Hawk in his. Whatever had happened between them—if anything had except an act for Alex Cordell's benefit on Hawk's side—it was definitely over now.

The Beresfords had kept to Tom's suite the majority of the time, and when Geraldine was taken into custody in London her husband was at her side. For all her faults, Tom seemed to be going to stand by her.

Hawk had driven Whitney to her home, refusing to come in, telling her they both needed breathing space to think where they went from here.

A week later she had still heard nothing from him. And with no job to go to either, she was quietly going out of her mind!

'What on earth do you think you're doing?'

She almost fell from her precarious perch on the window-ledge, showering the man that stood in the street below with water from the plastic can she held in her hand. 'Sorry!' She grimaced at Martin's indignant shout as he brushed the water off his jacket. 'But you shouldn't have frightened me like that.'

Martin squinted as the sun shone in his eyes as he looked up at her. 'Aren't you frightened of falling?'

'No,' she laughed as she edged back into the room, sticking her head back out to look at him once she was safely inside. 'Are you coming in or shall we just continue to shout at each other like this?' she derided.

'Very funny.' He stood in front of the door waiting for her to come and open it.

She had no idea why Martin had managed to pry himself from his desk long enough to come and visit her, but after seeing no one for a week she didn't particularly care, and dragged him inside.

'Hey,' he protested as he had no choice but to follow her up the stairs. 'I'm a married man!'

'Sorry,' she grimaced. 'Make yourself comfortable while I go and wash the dirt from my hands.'

Martin's wariness had gone by the time she joined him in what was obviously a lounge. He looked a little sheepish. 'I thought for a minute——'

'I know exactly what you thought,' she laughed.

'That my luck had changed!' He grinned.

She gave him a chiding look. 'You were terrified!'

'No, I——' He broke off, his expression rueful. 'I don't have the energy to keep up with a youngster like you,' he acknowledged. 'Tempted though I might be to try, I'm comfortable with my wife.'

'Comfortable' may sound dull to some people, but Whitney could only guess at the love and caring that progressed a marriage to that depth of intimate feeling. It sounded wonderful. But it would never be hers, because she would never have Hawk.

'What were you doing when I arrived?' Martin frowned.

'Watering my garden.' She indicated the flower boxes outside the window.

'Ah.' He nodded understanding, stretching out in one of the arm chairs. 'Nice place you have here.' He looked around approvingly.

'I like it.' She nodded, watching him warily; Martin didn't usually have the time or the patience for social pleasantries!

He returned her gaze with narrowed eyes. 'How have you been?'

'Fine.'

'You don't look it,' he told her with the brutal honesty that was typical of him.

She had missed Hawk more than ever this last week, and the dark shadows beneath her eyes told their own story, as did the way her jeans hung loosely on her hips. Food held no interest for her, and she had 'spring-cleaned' the house from top to bottom in an effort to keep busy and expend some energy. The combination of the two had left her pale and thin.

'Did Hawk send you?' she asked half resentfully, half hopefully.

'Only indirectly,' he shrugged.

She frowned. 'How indirectly?'

'I asked him when you were coming back to work,' Martin explained. 'He told me to come and find out.'

Whitney's frown deepened. 'But I no longer have a job on the *National*.'

'Since when?'

'Since Hawk dismissed me!'

Martin shook his head. 'He hasn't dismissed you. I'm your editor, I should know!'

'But—where did you think I've been for the last week and a half?' she demanded incredulously.

Martin suddenly looked embarrased, and for a hard-bitten newspaper man that wasn't easy to do. 'Hawk told me the two of you were having a holiday together,' he explained awkwardly. 'It was a statement, not a request, and it isn't my business to question his decisions.'

Hawk hadn't sacked her at all; he intended her returning to work as soon as they got back from Amsterdam! Only he hadn't bothered to tell *her* that, damn him.

'Well?' Martin prompted at her continued silence. 'Obviously things haven't worked out between you and Hawk, but you still have a job to go to.'

Amazing as it might seem, she realised that was

true. She felt anger at Hawk for his high-handed treatment of her, and relief that she didn't have to spend another aimless day around the house.

'Obviously you've missed the main Beresford/Cordell story.' Martin shrugged. 'But in the circumstances maybe you were too close to it to be objective.'

She wished she could agree with him, but in fact she hadn't been close to the real story at all, had completely misjudged the situation. Besides, Bill Summers had done an excellent job on the story; she knew she couldn't possibly have done better.

'But we do have the exclusive rights to Geraldine Beresford's side of the story,' Martin put in softly.

Whitney gave him a sharp look. 'She hasn't been charged?'

Martin shrugged. 'Not so far. And I doubt that she will.'

'But she's as guilty——'

'As her husband was?' He quirked mocking eyebrows.

Whitney flushed. 'OK, so I made a mistake about that. But Geraldine really is guilty; she admitted as much.'

Martin nodded. 'She's admitted carrying the drugs, but the police are convinced she did it unwittingly.'

'With people like Tom Beresford and—and Hawk behind her, I'm not surprised!' she said disgustedly.

'You're claws are showing, Whitney,' Martin

drawled. 'Why don't you listen to her side of the story before drawing any conclusions?'

'Me?' she echoed incredulously.

He nodded. 'She's insisted you be the reporter to do the interview. You have an appointment with her in'—he looked at his wristwatch—'half an hour.'

'Why didn't you say so?' She sprang into action. 'I have to change. I have to——'

'God save me from a woman getting ready to go out.' He stood up determinedly. 'Just be at the Beresfords by two-thirty,' he warned.

'You can count on it,' she assured him fervently.

After days of inactivity it felt good to have something cerebral to do, and she was interested in hearing what Geraldine had to say. Obviously the other woman wanted to speak to her again, too.

The housekeeper opened the door to her ring, but Whitney had noticed the two men outside the house; obviously the new 'minders'. Tom and Geraldine were going to need their privacy protected more than ever now that Geraldine was involved in a court case concerning drugs, even if it was only as the star witness.

Geraldine seemed to have changed in some way when she joined Whitney in the lounge a few minutes later. She was still as beautiful, her eyes still as hard, her control still coolly confident, but some of the brittleness seemed to have gone from her manner.

'I suppose you imagined I would be behind

bars by now?' she derided mockingly, indicating
for the housekeeper to put the tray on the coffee-
table.

'One can always hope,' Whitney returned tartly.

The green eyes softened with amusement. 'I
doubt the two of us will ever be friends.'

Whitney doubted it, too; in fact she didn't even
think it was a possibility!

Geraldine's mouth twisted. 'Thank God—
hmm?' she prompted derisively.

'My father said you were a man's woman,' she
shrugged. 'I doubt that will ever change.'

Geraldine sobered at the mention of Whitney's
father. 'Dan,' she sighed regretfully. 'I really
liked him, you know.'

'So you said,' Whitney nodded tersely.

'But you don't give a damn how I feel about
anything or anyone,' Geraldine guessed self-
derisively.

'I'm here to do an interview, Geraldine, not go
over old history,' she reminded tersely.

Geraldine sat back on the sofa after pouring
their tea, crossing one silky leg over the other.
'Go ahead,' she invited.

'Before we start, how is your husband now?'
she frowned.

'Much better, thank you. I'm making sure he
doesn't overdo things now.'

Whitney studied the other woman closely,
noting a slight softening in Geraldine's manner at
the mention of her husband. Maybe she really
did love the man, although it certainly wasn't
Whitney's idea of love.

She plunged on with the questions she had hurriedly written down before leaving home, amazed—and shocked—at the candidness of some of Geraldine's replies.

Two hours later she had so much information written down her head was buzzing with it all. And she still had one more question to ask.

'Now that you know your present husband's first wife died of a drugs overdose, and your first husband's best friend died in the same way, how do you feel about your lover's use of you?' She put the question in with a casualness she was far from feeling, her hands shaking slightly as she waited for the answer.

'I've always despised the abuse of drugs because of the way Dan died,' Geraldine answered hardly. 'Knowing Alex was involved in his death, and that of Tom's first wife, I can only hate him.'

Whitney's hands stopped shaking as she suddenly went numb, a ringing in her ears.

'Whitney?' Geraldine crossed the room to her side as she realised Whitney had made no effort to write her answer down as she had the others, her gaze accusing as she saw how pale Whitney had become. 'You tricked me,' she realised impatiently.

'Hawk wouldn't tell me the truth, and I——' She broke off, breathing hard, numbed at having confirmed the question that had been nagging at her ever since Hawk had explained his involvement in trying to arrest Alex Cordell. 'Why?' she groaned.

'Why what?' Geraldine came down on her haunches beside her, watching her anxiously.

'My father despised those sort of drugs and what they could do to you.' She shook her head disbelievingly.

Geraldine turned away. 'I'm not in a position to answer those questions, Whitney.'

'Why not?' she demanded. 'You know the truth, don't you?'

'Yes. But——' She sighed. 'I would have thought Hawk would have told you everything by now. The two of you are lovers——'

'Not any more.' She shook her head bitterly.

Geraldine frowned. 'What do you mean?'

'It was just an act,' she dismissed impatiently. 'To fool Alex Cordell into believing he was in no danger of exposure from me.'

'You and Hawk weren't lovers?' Geraldine said slowly.

Colour darkened her cheeks. 'Not at first, no,' she said heavily.

'But after we came on board?' the other woman encouraged.

'Yes,' she sighed.

'Then why——I'm going to telephone Hawk.' Geraldine straightened decisively.

'No!'

'But, Whitney——'

'Thank you for the interview, Geraldine,' she told her abruptly. 'You've been very helpful. But I do have to go now.'

Geraldine followed her to the door. 'There's so much you still don't know,' she tried to tell her.

'I know all I need to—all I *want* to,' she said emotionally.

'But you can't,' Geraldine shook her head. 'You can't know that I lied to you about Hawk's reason for giving up racing, that it had nothing to do with his guardianship of you, that after your father's death he decided it wasn't worth the pain and heartache——'

'It doesn't matter,' she dismissed dully. 'None of it matters.'

'But it does,' the other woman insisted frustratedly. 'Hawk's been in love with you for years, and now he's doing nothing about it!'

'You're wrong,' Whitney said bitterly.

'I *know* he loves you,' Geraldine rasped.

'You misunderstood me,' she told her wearily. '*However* Hawk feels about me, he *is* doing something about it—he's dismissed me from his life!'

'I never realised how stupid he was,' Geraldine said disgustedly.

Whitney gave her a wan smile. 'We both know that Hawk always knows exactly what he's doing.'

'And right now he's being stupid,' Geraldine rasped. 'My God, you're no longer a child, and it's time he realised it! I've never liked you, Whitney——But it wasn't personal,' she added, receiving a snort of derision from Whitney. 'I would have resented anyone who intruded on my life with Hawk. He was never really happy with me, but at first I did try to be the sort of wife I thought he needed. And then you came along, the daughter of his best friend. It could all have been so different,' she sighed. 'We could have been a family, you could have been the daughter I lost——'

'You told me you didn't want that!' Whitney protested.

Geraldine's mouth twisted. 'I only needed to take one look at you to know it couldn't be like that. Even at fifteen you were beautiful, and you obviously worshipped Hawk——'

'I loved him for being kind to me, that was all,' she defended.

Geraldine nodded. 'He could never have been any other way with you.'

'Because he's always "kind to children and animals",' she said bitterly.

'Don't be ridiculous,' the other woman snapped. 'Oh, that's true, too, but it wasn't the reason Hawk was so good with you. He wanted you even then.'

'Now who's being ridiculous?'

Geraldine shook her head sadly. 'I know what I'm talking about, Whitney,' she said confidently. 'Just as I know Hawk tried to fight his feelings for you. He even tried to resume our physical relationship, but it didn't work out,' she added at Whitney's pained gasp. 'After that I became even more determined to keep the two of you apart; I wasn't going to be ousted from my position as his wife by a mere child!'

'You aren't doing anything to keep us apart now,' she derided hardly. 'And we still aren't together.' She turned to leave.

'But you haven't heard what I did to keep you apart,' Geraldine called after her. 'Whitney, listen to me——'

'I'm sorry,' she shook her head. 'I really do have to go.'

'But——'

'Goodbye, Geraldine,' she cut in firmly. 'I should try and hang on to Tom Beresford; he seems like a good man.'

'I'm going to, and he is,' Geraldine nodded. 'But——' Her mouth compressed as Whitney walked away.

Whitney didn't give herself time to think. She went straight to the *National* building, entering Martin's office after only the briefest of knocks, and dropped her notebook on to his desk.

'What——!' He stared at the chaos the notebook had made of the rest of the papers on his desk. 'What do you think you're doing?' he demanded angrily.

'That's my notes on my interview with Geraldine Beresford,' she told him coldly. 'I've decided I can't do the story after all, I'm too personally involved.'

'But—whitney, what's going on?' He looked at her with narrowed eyes.

'Ask Hawk,' she sighed. 'He has all the answers. Although he's a little reticent about giving them,' she added bitterly.

'Stop talking in riddles,' Martin snapped.

'I resign—is that clear enough?' She glared at him fiercely.

'Very clear,' he spluttered. 'Although it doesn't tell me the reason why.'

She shook her head. 'I don't have to give that.'

'What about working your notice? Whitney, you can't just walk out——'

'I'm sure Hawk will forgo my notice,' she scoffed. 'Take it up with him,' she dismissed carelessly. '*He* could write the story better than anyone!'

'This is ridiculous,' Martin said exasperatedly. 'Are you telling me you're walking out on a perfectly good job because you're angry with Hawk?'

Her eyes flashed. 'I'm more than angry with him,' she scorned. 'I despise him!'

'Now you know that isn't true——'

'The man has treated me as no better than an idiot since we first met,' she told him furiously. 'I want nothing more to do with him; I don't even want to work for him!'

'Whitney——'

For the second time that day she walked out on someone in the middle of a conversation, her head held high as she walked through the room full of her fellow reporters, keeping a tight control on her emotions as she had since Geraldine had so unwittingly revealed the truth about her father that Hawk had chosen to keep from her.

But once she reached her home she couldn't hold back the tears any longer. Her father, the fun-loving man she had loved so much, had died because he had become addicted to the drugs

Alex Cordell supplied to him. Oh, she realised
that if her father were determined to obtain the
drugs, as only an addict can be, that he would
have got them from someone else if Alex Cordell
hadn't sold them to him. But that didn't stop her
hating the man with a violence completely alien
to her. And she despised Hawk for letting her
find out the truth in such a way.

She heard the banging on the door downstairs
as if from a great distance, her mouth tightening,
her body stiffening resentfully as she guessed it
had to be Hawk demanding entrance in such an
arrogant manner. She had no intention of talking
to him, so——

She came abruptly to her feet as she heard the
splintering of wood and a loud crash as the forced
door flew back against the wall.

Her eyes were wide with apprehension as
Hawk's body filled the doorway.

And then she chided herself for showing him
anything but contempt, flames shooting across
the room at him from her violet eyes.

He seemed to relax a little as he saw the
antagonism in her eyes, strolling casually into the
room, looking for all the world as if he hadn't just
forced his way into her home by breaking her
door down. 'Half of London seems to be
concerned about you,' he bit out.

Hawk was verbally attacking *her*; that was the
last thing she had been expecting!

'I've had Geraldine on the telephone telling me
what a fool I am,' he continued grimly. 'And
Martin shouting across my desk at me that I've

ruined not only your life but your career, too.' He looked at her with narrowed eyes.

Whitney glared at him. 'Why couldn't you have told me about my father? Why did you——'

'Because I love you.'

'. . . let me go on thinking——?' She broke off dazedly as his answer penetrated her anger. 'What did you say?' she gasped.

Hawk winced at her obvious disbelief. 'I said I love you.'

She watched him warily now. 'I don't believe it,' she finally told him forcefully. No man in love with a woman could have treated her the way Hawk had.

'No,' he accepted heavily. 'Although it's the truth. I'm too damned old for you; I have one unsuccessful marriage behind me; but I do love you.'

Whitney still looked at him with suspicion as she began to pace the room, stopping briefly to look at him before resuming her pacing. 'I know how my father died,' she rasped.

'I know,' he nodded. 'And I'm sorry you had to find out the way you did.'

'*You* could have told me,' she accused. 'Years ago.'

He was suddenly very pale. 'How do you tell a fifteen-year-old who had just lost the only parent she had left, and whom she obviously adored, that, because he had to be a winner, the only way he could still race with the pain he still suffered from the accident that nearly killed him the year before was to take drugs to drive out that pain?'

'Drugs helped him do that?' Whitney gasped.

'For a while,' Hawk nodded grimly. 'And then he started taking them because he couldn't get through a day without them. I tried to get him to stop but he wouldn't listen to me. His reflexes became so dulled by the drugs in the end that by that last race he didn't even try to turn the corner, he just went straight into the wall and the bike went up in flames.'

Whitney shuddered at this graphic account of her father's self-destruction. 'You still shouldn't have kept it from me. I was old enough——'

'If you had been you would never have become my ward,' Hawk scorned. 'The first time I held you, at the school, after telling you about Dan, I knew I could be a danger to you. I was supposed to be a father figure to you, and all I could think about was making love to you!' he groaned self-disgustedly.

'You never showed that by a single word or gesture,' she protested.

'You'll never know the willpower it took not to,' he rasped. 'Geraldine wasn't fooled for a minute. She took one look at us together and knew exactly what was happening to me. I suppose because she knew I didn't love her she was able to recognise when I did fall in love,' he said grimly. 'It wasn't just the age difference that stood between us, there was my marriage, and for a while I tried to get that back on a normal footing. It was a fiasco; I didn't want Geraldine, just as I haven't wanted any other woman but

you the last seven years. Geraldine was angry at
this second rejection, wasn't averse to using that
anger to turn my feelings against me.'

Whitney frowned at his bitterness. 'What do
you mean?'

He shrugged, his hands thrust into his trouser
pockets. 'I made the mistake of giving her
tangible proof of my love for you!'

Whitney became suddenly still, her anger
having faded long ago. 'How?'

'For three years I had you as my friend, my
companion, and—and when the time came to let
you go I—I found I couldn't do it. Don't look at
me like that, Whitney,' he snapped as she
frowned her confusion. 'Don't you realise? There
was no age of twenty-one mentioned in your
father's will, only the age of consent, which we all
know is eighteen. I kept you in my house, as my
ward, three years longer than I should have
done!'

Her brow cleared as the significance of that
washed over her. It had been shortly after her
eighteenth birthday that Geraldine began to go
her own way in the marriage, when Hawk had
seemed to withdraw into himself. Geraldine had
said earlier that she had set out to keep them
apart; had the knowledge of what Hawk had done
been the method she used to achieve that? But
how? It still didn't make sense to her.

'Hawk, you had to know by then how I felt
about you, that guardianship or no guardianship
I would have continued to live with you anyway
if you had asked me.'

He sighed. 'I knew you imagined yourself in love with me——'

'It was never *imagined*!' she denied hotly.

'It didn't make any difference.' He shook his head. 'Geraldine was angry about my feelings for you, as she had a right to be. She wanted to live her own life, within the confines of our marriage, and she told me that if I attempted to divorce her she would name *you* as my lover. I didn't care for myself, but I couldn't have your life ruined because of a love you had no knowledge of.'

What Geraldine had done to keep her marriage intact until *she* decided to end it had been cruel, but even as she realised that Whitney acknowledged that probably any wife, in the same circumstances, would feel bitter enough about her husband's love for a younger woman to do the same thing. Whitney had a feeling she would be capable of such cruelty if the husband were Hawk!

'Surely all that changed once she decided to marry Tom Beresford?' she accused.

'I was deeply involved in catching Alex Cordell by that time, too deeply involved to want you anywhere near him,' he said grimly.

He had explained so much of what had hurt her over the years, and yet he still couldn't seem to accept that she was no longer a child to be protected, from himself or anyone else. 'I could have worked with you on that instead of fighting against you if you had only confided in me!'

'You did help me.' His gaze held hers, his eyes very golden. 'For two days—and two un-forgettable nights!—you loved me.'

'It wasn't just for two days, or two nights,' she protested. 'I've always loved you, and I always will. And you let me go on thinking you were still in love with Geraldine.'

'In the circumstances it seemed the best thing to do——'

'Best for *whom*?' she exploded indignantly. 'You? Because it certainly wasn't best for me! I've been living in misery this last year thinking that you didn't want me in your life now that your *duty* was done!'

'I couldn't keep you with me at the house once Geraldine had gone.' He shook his head.

'My God, do you realise that each time we've made love I thought I was a substitute for her!'

'I never loved her,' he told Whitney softly. 'Not even at the beginning.'

Whitney nodded impatiently. 'She told me the circumstances behind your marriage. But *you* should have been the one to explain that, to tell me about my father, too. How can you say you love me with one breath and yet still treat me like a child that needs protecting from life the next?'

His mouth twisted. 'My marriage to Geraldine happened long before you came into my life. As for telling you about your father, I didn't have the right to deprive you of that illusion, too!'

'You would rather someone else did it!'

'No,' he groaned. 'I had hoped you need never have to know the truth about that. You loved the man, Whitney,' he reasoned forcefully. 'Maybe I was wrong, but I didn't feel there was any need to ruin the memories you've always had of him.'

He hadn't been wrong, she knew he hadn't, knew that now she knew the truth about her father's accident she would never feel the same about it again.

'None of this explains your absence from my life this last week,' she accused, still angry about that at least.

'No,' he sighed, running a hand through the thickness of his hair. 'I took advantage of you aboard the *Freedom*——'

Her disbelieving laugh interrupted him. 'I practically threw myself at you!'

'Not that first time——'

'*All* the time,' she rebuked.

He shook his head. 'You were frightened——'

'Not enough to make love with a man I didn't love!' Her eyes flashed.

Hawk sighed. 'Maybe you won't believe this, but I couldn't have stayed away much longer,' he admitted. 'While you were just the beautiful young woman who was once my ward—and that I loved beyond comprehension!—I could live with it. But once we made love——! I can't stay away from you, Whitney!' he groaned achingly. 'You're as necessary to me as the air I breathe.'

'And what happens now?' She glared at him.

He shrugged. 'I think that's up to you. Geraldine may have been acting out of pain and anger, but she's right about the speculation there will be if you marry me.'

'She would still carry out that threat?' Whitney frowned.

Hawk shook his head. 'That bitterness is gone,

at least. But our story would be newsworthy, Whitney. I can just see the headlines now: "Beautiful Young Ward Marries Man Who Was Her Guardian".' His mouth twisted.

'Would it bother you?' She watched him closely.

'God, no,' he dismissed derisively. 'It's always been your reputation I've been concerned about. If I could have you as my wife I wouldn't care what they called me!'

'You're arrogant, domineering, irritating, totally inconsiderate—but I'll still love you until the day I die,' she choked. 'And scandal or no scandal, I intend to marry you.' She met his gaze unflinchingly as he raised his brows mockingly at her own domineering arrogance. 'If you refuse, *I'll* tell everyone you seduced me!' she warned.

'It isn't nice to remind me of the weakness I have for you,' he drawled, his eyes glowing.

'It's your choice,' she challenged, tension holding her body taut.

His expression softened, his arms moving possessively about her. 'I'm fifteen years older than you, have made more mistakes in my thirty-seven years than I care to think about—most of them concerning you, it seems.' He frowned. 'I really will try not to protect you so much, Whitney,' he promised gruffly. 'But it's difficult when I just want to wrap you up in cotton wool.'

She knew it would take time and patience for Hawk to realise just how independent she had become this last year, but she also knew that he would finally come to realise she was his partner in life and no longer a responsibility. A few more nights together like the ones they had spent on the *Freedom* and he would be in no doubt of her maturity!

'You still haven't answered my proposal,' she reminded.

'If you want me I'm yours,' he told her intently. 'I've always been yours!'

And strangely she knew that he had, felt as if they had always belonged together. It had been a stormy crossing to this point in their lives; she could only hope that the years ahead would be smoother for them.

Although she wouldn't count on it. They promised to be the happiest years of their lives!

Harlequin Presents

Coming Next Month

Available in March wherever paperback books are sold, or through Harlequin Reader Service:

In the U.S.
P.O. Box 1397
Buffalo, N.Y.
14240-1397

In Canada
P.O. Box 603
Fort Erie, Ontario
L2A 5X3

Take 4 best-selling love stories FREE

Plus get a FREE surprise gift!

Six exciting series
for you every month...
from Harlequin

Harlequin Romance·
The series that started it all

Tender, captivating and heartwarming...
love stories that sweep you off to faraway places
and delight you with the magic of love.

♦

Harlequin Presents·
Powerful contemporary love
stories...as individual as the
women who read them

The No. 1 romance series...
exciting love stories for you, the woman of today...
a rare blend of passion and dramatic realism.

♦

Harlequin Superromance®
It's more than romance...
it's Harlequin Superromance

A sophisticated, contemporary romance-fiction
series, providing you with a longer,
more involving read...a richer mix of complex plots,
realism and adventure.

Harlequin American Romance™
Harlequin celebrates the American woman...

...by offering you romance stories written about American women, by American women for American women. This series offers you contemporary romances uniquely North American in flavor and appeal.

◆

Harlequin Temptation™
Passionate stories for today's woman

An exciting series of sensual, mature stories of love...dilemmas, choices, resolutions... all contemporary issues dealt with in a true-to-life fashion by some of your favorite authors.

◆

Harlequin Intrigue
Because romance can be quite an adventure

Harlequin Intrigue, an innovative series that blends the romance you expect... with the unexpected. Each story has an added element of intrigue that provides a new twist to the Harlequin tradition of romance excellence.

◆

Harlequin Books

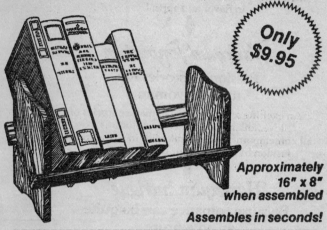